BOOK 2 OF THE SANCTUARY CHRONICLES

GREG RODE

ISBN: 978-1-954614-37-6

Rode. Greg
One

Edited by: Melissa Long
Illustrations by: Merissa Jones

Published by Warren Publishing
Charlotte, NC
www.warrenpublishing.net
Printed in the United States

To my family, near and far, who have been
along for the whole ride. I am deeply
thankful for your support, especially
in these months of my own adventure.

Also for Jessica Pieloch.
Thank you for the elephant.
I really needed that,
more than you know.

There is power in a name.
                    -TSE WAI LEE

I sit on the front porch of what I've always thought of as my grandparents' cabin, though they are long gone. The cabin lies on the shore of a small mountain lake, a peaceful oasis for much of my life until now. My shotgun rests against the dark wooden railing in front of me, and one of my well-used .45 handguns is on my right thigh. I've got a tumbler of whiskey close to hand, though no rocks, no twist. The dog sits with me, curled at my feet in a glowing ray of sunlight.

I am waiting.

I am ready.

CHAPTER 1

The trip to Pennsylvania and, ultimately, upstate New York is going to take ages, of course. After blowing the zombies to smithereens in Huntersville, North Carolina, we left immediately, anxious to leave the horrors and memories behind us. Part of me is reluctant to leave the relative safety of the compact compound I have built over the past months, but most of me recognizes that there is now probably too much baggage there and a fresh start will perhaps do us all some good.

I feel some fleeting guilt about Jack's death, but there was no alternative; sooner or later, it would've come to a head. At least I gave him (something of) a fighting chance. I struggle some with the idea that I have contributed to the death of one of the few remaining humans, but it isn't like there had been any ambiguity about Jack's character—he was a conniving, selfish asshole. The women asked no real questions about my solitary return after the explosion, probably being content with the explanation I had given—that Jack had gone down fighting—and wanting to know nothing more. All of them had good reason to wish him gone as well, so we moved on. This is the only thing we can do now; the past, along with virtually everything else, is water under the bridge.

We have our mammoth, black Ford truck, loaded with guns, ammo, extra gas cans, food, sleeping bags, ammo, guns, water jugs, maps, tools, guns, and ammo. Did I mention we have a few guns and some ammo?

Waiter, I'd like an order of guns, a side of ammo, and hold the zombies, please.

Yes, I do think I need some sleep.

We also carry a slim measure of hope with us that somehow, amidst the dying of the world as we know it, Eve's and my families survived. I'm sure we're mixing a dose of reality in with that hope since the plague of the zombies swept through the Charlotte area, at least, and wiped out a million-plus people in what felt like the blink of an eye. Certainly, the other large cities are just as devastated, but Eve's family lives in the smallish town of Lake Ariel, Pennsylvania, in the northern central part of the state. So she desperately hopes they've been isolated enough to avoid the carnage, infection, and annihilation. The Pocono Mountains wind through that part, as does Interstate-81, which is ideal since that is the route we need to take to my family's land in the Catskills. The town is east of the highway by just a few miles and it's not like we're on any kind of schedule. The world is our oyster—albeit infested with the damn, flesh-eating hordes. At least we've done something of our part by killing nearly fifty of them in one lovely, noisy, dynamite-fed hail of nail shrapnel.

Occupying my free time over the past months included sweeping the nearby roads clean of abandoned cars and trucks so I could drive freely at any rate of speed I chose. Driving has long soothed me, especially in my teenage years when I just needed time to sort everything out that tortured the minds of teens. I'm also terrible at relaxing, so the gargantuan mess that has been thrown at us has, in its own weird way, luckily given me a giant to-do list, which keeps my mind mostly off the new reality and, instead, on the task of survival.

I have only cleared the highway down to Charlotte, back to the south, and for a dozen miles or so to the north. There weren't too many vehicles out on the roads—most people had hidden at home without knowing they were just waiting to die—but there are some atrocious, multi-dozen vehicle wrecks north of Mooresville that are even worse than the ones on a summer Friday afternoon; we will have to navigate those. The truck—or maybe I should say "TRUCK," though I already do that with the KNIFE, so mayhap I should not get carried away—is a four-wheel drive, and a winch is mounted on the delightful black, iron push bar mounted over the front bumper. We'll be able to go around, drag away, or push through almost anything.

For the first time, I truly appreciate my neighbors' choices of vehicles since this was not my truck but rather one of my scavenging finds. The towns north of Charlotte are largely filled with the well-to-do and there are an astonishing number of exotic cars and high-end SUVs whose capabilities vastly exceed the abilities of their owners. Does your typical banker *need* a $100,000 Porsche or BMW for the commute to downtown, rolling at a steady twenty-five miles an hour, or does his stay-at-home spouse require a car that can do everything incredibly fast, such as going to the grocery store or tennis lessons or a nail salon? Of course not, but some of that is what has made Americans so very "American," and I'm now the beneficiary of some of that excess.

The full trip is almost seven hundred miles on the button from Huntersville to my family's lake house and property in New York, with the side trip to check on Eve's family. I assume we'll average no better than thirty miles an hour for the duration, but I also figure we'll do some exploring along the way when it's time to stop for gas or the necessaries.

Realistically, I doubt we'll run into any remaining shreds of civilization along the way, but I think we may run into other bands of survivors like us, which can be a good or bad thing. We're certainly capable of defending ourselves, but one man with three women—one a middle teen and the others attractive adults—can draw unwelcome interest. We'll have to be careful. The rules that existed before do not exist now.

Regardless of what we find at Lake Ariel, we're going to upstate New York afterward for a handful of reasons. It's absolutely in the middle of nowhere, which reduces the likely count of zombie neighbors; the cabins back up to the shore of a lake, so one side will be protected; the winters are utterly miserable, which will shrink the time when we have to be alert; and I know every square inch of the area from vacationing in the summers growing up. There are no nts in the dozen or so cabins that sprinkle the area, and it's not like there have been very many people moving to upstate New York over the past few decades, so it should be lightly-populated with anything, if anything. There will be more than enough room for us, and if we are fortunate enough to find some of Eve's family, we can accommodate them as well.

I haven't been there in close to a decade after moving away from southern New York to the Charlotte area after my grandparents passed, but I can visualize everything as easily as when I saw it through my ten-year-old eyes. It's a place that barely changes, is blissfully peaceful—though some of that may be due to the remnants of a child's memory tucked away in my mind—should be fairly defensible without significant effort, and where we should be able to survive.

With DeeDee beside me, Amelie and Eve in the back seats, and our supplies occupying the entire bed of the truck, we set off to the North, hoping it brings something—anything—better. My first road trip in many moons is sure to be like none I have ever taken before.

**

For the most part, the early part of the trip through the northern part of North Carolina that leads toward the Virginia border is uneventful. We see no other moving cars, no people, no zombies. The scattered detritus of humanity is evident everywhere, as is the occasional sighting of corpses along the road mixed with the abandoned cars standing with doors open in welcome for an owner who is long dead

... or undead. Safe to say the "new car smell" is a thing of the past and the "zombie car smell" is now all the rage. Carrion birds drift above it all, floating in the thermal drafts with little effort, occasionally dropping to the ground for a snack. Good eating for them, this.

In the past, it took me roughly two hours to reach the mountains that climb to the divide between the states; it now takes a little fewer than four as we make our way around wrecks that litter the roadway, but, otherwise, we make fair progress. All the women sleep quietly for the most part, though Amelie is periodically restless and mumbles in her sleep. It's hard to imagine what this all feels like for someone so young, who hasn't yet been run over by some of life's harder realities and retains the optimism of youth that life is great, aside from not-very-serious boy stuff. Parents gone, friends gone, creatures from the movies overrunning everything, and danger at every turn. Not to mention her oddball collection of adopted new family. Who knows what she thinks of us: the rough-edged but soft-hearted ex-something—Dancer? Cocktail waitress? Stripper? Other?—in DeeDee, the reserved and peaceful Eve who holds most everything inside, and me, the protector and provider; not exactly your classic suburban family unit. But all of us have been strong enough to survive so far, whether it has been the obscene demands of the zombie queen and her horde of monsters, or the poison that Jack's presence brought into the house. We're able to lean evermore on one another.

***

One of two things will happen as you begin the climb on the interstate up into the mountains—well, "mountains" by East Coast standards—that separate the two states. Either it's brilliantly clear and affords a spectacular view off to the east, or the fog is in and it's a matter of degrees for how soupy it will be. I've been on this road in the past at a literal crawl with my hazard lights on, both for something to cut through the dense fog that clings to the pavement with wispy tentacles and to minimize the chances of being rear-ended by a hero in an SUV. Visibility can be as low as ten to twenty feet in front of you, cutting off the rest of the world in a haze that just hints of reality outside of arm's reach.

Today is one of those days, so I drop the speed from a blazing forty miles an hour down to ten and flip the hazards on. I feel the fatigue in my eyes as I strain to see as far forward as I can, knowing the chances of a vacant car across the road or a jack-knifed tractor trailer—which will force us to retrace our steps and attempt the southbound lanes for the crossing—is pretty high. Despite the lack of rules, I still find myself driving on the right side of the road for the most part—old habits die harder than the world did.

The next mile creeps by like a Friday afternoon at work before happy hour and a golf vacation. I realize we're going to need to change drivers soon, or I'll be really testing the off-road abilities of this truck the hard way.

As I round the next curve, I see them. A lot of them. A shitload of them strewn across the road and blocking it from the guardrail over to where the asphalt runs out and the natural stone begins its steep rise to the sky. There is nowhere to pass on either side. On, off, on, off in the blink of the amber hazard lights. At least fifty of them, the goddamn zombies that have been the plague of humanity's existence and the near-constant thorn in my side for the past year or so. I stop the truck in the center of the two lanes and put the transmission into "Park," sensing the women awakening from the suspension of motion.

"Ladies, make sure the doors are all locked. We've got company, and a lot of it," I say as I watch DeeDee rub her eyes sleepily.

"Jesus, look at all them fuckers," she yawns, though without much more amazement than if she'd seen a handful of cows on the side of the road.

We're all fairly numb to the existence of actual zombies running wild all over the world. The world had become desensitized to violence, language, horror, and other insanities before all of this happened. Zombie movies and television shows were beyond prevalent. Kids dressed as them for Halloween. Zombies were *cool*.

Zombies are not cool.

They're horrid abominations of nature or God or science, pick your poison. They're creatures who eat people, tearing them to shreds in the process. They have no "Off" button, no pause, no commercials. They never stop coming. They have no mercy. They kill or die, nothing else. They're a black wave of death that's killed everyone. Everyone but us four, for all we know.

"Then fire whenever you're ready. Once you start, I'm sure they'll scatter or attack, more likely attack, so shoot until the truck starts moving and then drop back in so I can close the roof. We'll just drive through them and go on our way, but taking a few out is always a good idea." I set the truck back into "Drive" and tighten my seatbelt firmly across my waist and shoulder like I did outside the dynamite shop, not wanting to bash my head off the roof of the truck again. I see Eve and DeeDee doing the same.

It all happens quickly enough that I'm not sure I see everything perfectly. Just as I hear Amelie breathe out quietly, I see the Pats jersey melt backward into the crowd, and I think I see him push two other zombies between himself and the truck. Her first shot spatters the head of one of them into a fine cloud of finger-sized pieces of gore, and then her second catches Lefty just below the noggin, tearing nearly half his neck clean off. As I pull my eyes away from the sight of its head drooping suddenly to the side, I see the jersey again and shout for Amelie to try for him.

Muuuuuuuhhhhh!

They all shout at the same time, louder than I've ever heard, and I can see the main zombie pushing the others toward the truck, urging them forward to attack us.

Dammit. That's two of them we've seen acting as leaders, and two feels like a pattern. A very unpleasant pattern.

"Amelie, drop in, here we go!" I shout as I let my foot off the brake and drill the loud pedal. The truck surges forward to meet the mass of gelatinous ex-humans, and I hear a thump as Amelie hits the back seat. "DeeDee, get the

roof!" She holds the switch as the gap between the truck and the charging mass shrinks to just a few feet. "Hang on!" I'm doing a lot of shouting here, but I'm trying to keep my eye on my target through the crowd and the dissipating fog. If we can't shoot him, we're going to run his ass over with a couple of tons of Detroit steel at thirty miles an hour. Then, I may back up over him to be on the safe side.

The front bumper hits the first couple of zombies, spraying the hood and windshield with their murky blood. In the precious second or two that it takes me to turn the wipers and washers on, I lose sight of the jersey, and then we're in the middle of them. Bodies pelt against the sides and front of the big Ford as we meet the main bulk of the crowd. My driver's side mirror is torn away as it clips the head off one of our assailants. The speedometer passes thirty and sweeps toward forty as the chunky, off road tires crunch over a series of bodies, and we're rattled around in the cabin. The women are all shouting as the horrible decaying faces of the zombies appear and then vanish in the windows. Fists and arms pound on the vehicle as it passes through them, a motley crew of whoever used to live in this area and fell to the modern-day plague.

It's over in just a few seconds, though it feels like longer. We pass through the crowd and are out. No one is hurt—on our side anyway—and no damage is done to the truck that I can see other than my mirror, though I'm sure we have a bunch of new dents, and it will need a bath to clean off all the goo.

I stop a few hundred yards past the mess in the road, scanning the survivors for the Patriots jersey in case it's worth taking a shot or two or backing the truck up for another pass, but I see only chaos. The remaining mob is turning in our direction and stepping over the bodies of their fallen in pursuit, some of whom are moving and some not. I don't see him, so I turn back to the highway that spirals up the mountain and continue on our way. There are far too many of them in that group for us to kill them all, and my intent for this trip is to largely avoid direct conflicts unless we absolutely have to wherever possible, so we aren't taking any chances.

The truck seems unscathed, and a missing mirror isn't going to be a problem. There is nothing behind us anyway, just everything.

Several miles down the road, I hear a thumping noise from the bottom of the truck. Not a consistent, repetitive one like a flat tire, but an intermittent *bump, bump, bump*. I'm exhausted and know we really need to change drivers so I can rest, so I figure this is as good a reason as any to pull over and swap. We probably could stand to top off the gas from the plastic tanks in the bed, too, since this stretch of highway is pretty quiet for amenities, even during the best of times.

The flood of adrenaline has worn off, and I'm somewhere on the fringes of about my fifth wind and definitely not feeling sharp, so it shouldn't be surprising that I make another mistake.

I loathe mistakes, or at least ones I make. In my old life, I was good at my job, which was pretty sexy stuff. Data—the integrity of it, the control of the flow from one place to another, and analysis into what it told you. I would focus intensely on my work and was always very thoughtful and practical; I really knew my stuff. One of those times where the nature of the work and the worker were a good match: data arguably requires perfection, and I was, and still am, inarguably a perfectionist. It was rare that I made an error, but when I did, it would gnaw at me for days. However, that made me even better at the job since I'd have an even tighter attention to detail as a result. Mistakes are now a far more serious thing, and my recent ones have almost cost Amelie's innocence and my life. That bastard Jack—I just don't think the same way as other people, so I didn't foresee the depths of his twisted soul. I'm lucky he hadn't had time to coerce Amelie into intercourse with him and didn't have the balls to shoot me when he had the chance. Now, it's just fatigue that's getting me into trouble.

I take my foot off the gas and drift slowly to a stop over the course of the next few hundred yards. I'm still hearing the bumping sound at its random interval, so I don't think it's something mechanical. No need to pull off onto the shoulder.

"Do you all hear that or am I just shot?" I ask around the inside of the cabin.

"No, I hear it, though you do look like shit," Eve answers.

"Thanks, you're a pal, though I said 'shot,' not 'shit.' Glad you're there for me." I smile and Eve grins back at me. I set the truck into "Park" and release my seatbelt. "Who wants to drive next? I need some sleep, or we're not going to make it to Virginia even."

"Can I?" asks Amelie.

"Maybe not right here, but once we clear the fog and mountains, why not?" Not like anyone is going to care or notice, and as long as someone else is awake with her, this is about as easy as it gets. No one on the road, no cops, nada. Let's go crazy, party like it's 1999. What the hell, right?

I step out of the truck, left foot first, and that's when the rotten bastard grabs my ankle. Its grip is unbelievably strong, especially given that it has been dragging underneath a moving vehicle for a few miles. There's no way in hell it couldn't have been scraping the road. The human body is amazingly powerful, though our current culture doesn't do much to take advantage of this wonderful engine—too many of us used to sit on our asses all day at office jobs, and only a smaller portion of us would go to the gym to at least mimic the all-day work we used to do to survive. I'd heard the stories of the mothers lifting cars off their trapped children and junkies on PCP still coming at the police despite a half-dozen bullets in them, but I was skeptical until all of this happened. Having been face-to-face with these abominations too many times to recount, I know how shockingly strong a human body can become when driven by unending hunger and *rage*. I feel it here in the sharp, squeezing vice locked onto my leg. It starts pulling me toward the undercarriage, grasping fingertips digging into my jeans and surely drawing blood.

"Fuck! Gun, gun, gun!" I shout as I begin to lose my footing. I do not want to fight under a truck where I'll be at a horrible disadvantage. Space is your friend with these monsters, and gunpowder really is the greatest invention ever.

It gives another yank, and I go flat on my back with a jarring thud to my spine that is sure to be sore tomorrow, if I get to see tomorrow. My .45 handgun is on the front seat in between me and Eve; all I have is the KNIFE and a really lousy angle with which to use it now that my legs are mostly under the truck. Maybe I can bend and reach and slash across its hand, but things are quickly getting out of control as it drags me unrelentingly. I can see him now— it's the damned Pats jersey-wearing zombie, the king to our queen. His mouth yawns impossibly wide as he draws me in closer, just a foot to go before that terrible maw can close on me. I desperately try to find a handhold to keep from going all the way under.

Suddenly, a heavy weight hits me in the chest.

"Here!" screams Eve from above me. She has dived across the cab of the truck and dropped the pistol down where I can grab it.

I fumble with the gun with my left hand since my right is holding the door jamb. I finally turn the gun the right way and hope I've left the safety off. There are no little kids in the world that we've seen, and that split second between on and off is critical, so none of us usually leave the safety on, ever. Except Jack, and that worked out fine. For me, anyway.

The safety is off. I may have been tired-stupid, but at least I'm a little lucky.

I fire three quick shots between my feet at the zombie. His grip loosens after the first shot, so I may have hit him somewhere good. The second shot bounces off the pavement and slashes through the side of his face, leaving a deep furrow from mouth to ear. The third shot goes square through the nose.

The iron clamp on my ankle slackens, and I drag myself slowly out from underneath the truck, shaking with fear and anger. My ankle hurts like a sonofabitch, and I see a bit of blood seeping through the cuff of my jeans. I tell Eve to move the truck out of the way, which she does.

I stand over the dead, extra-dead, whatever dead, zombie. Since I've hit him in the face twice, there isn't much to look at there, and it looks like my first shot has pierced a hole in his chest. The rest of his visible skin is closer in shade to mine than the mottled, graying skin of the rest of them. It's just like the queen was—cleaner, newer, better. I shudder as I wonder if he has been eating infants.

I flip him over, feeling that I'm going to be moving gingerly for a while as I put pressure on my injured ankle and feel the strain in my back. His back is absolute hamburger from being dragged under the truck and his entire spine is shining brightly in the sun. What kind of thing is he that he can not only survive what should have been searing agony from the initial collision and the dragging, but also still retain his hold on the truck, just waiting for a chance to attack and eat?

One other thing comes to mind as I walk away from the corpse. I haven't thought about it much before, but I'm really going to miss football.

After limping back to the truck, I climb into the passenger seat so Eve can drive for a while. I assure the women I'm okay and rest my head back, feeling the adrenaline seep out of my system. Exhaustion quickly sets all the way in as I drift off to sleep, pondering the idea of alpha zombies.

Because the plain ones aren't entertaining enough.

Great.

CHAPTER 2

By the time I awaken, we're on Interstate-81 and have cleared all of Virginia somehow. Amelie is now at the wheel with the biggest smile I have ever seen on her face. She's grinning from ear to ear as she pilots the big truck along the highway at around forty miles an hour. I wonder if I had the same shit-eating grin when I first began to drive and figure everyone did after the initial nerves.

A bright thought—no football and for all we know, we've just had the last of the first-time drivers. I should talk to myself more often since I'm so damn cheerful here lately.

We eventually come to a wreck in the road. Amelie slows, edges onto the shoulder, and navigates smoothly around the twisted wreckage of an RV and 18-wheeler. It's messy, with glass and assorted bits and pieces of both vehicles strewn across the blacktop. One dead driver is leaning against the steering wheel of the RV.

Everyone seems content, though the light of the day is fading and I don't really want to be on the road during the night—just better to be safe than sorry. We should get some rest and avoid any chance of running into a stray deer or zombie on the road at night. One of the roadside signs says that Harrisburg, Pennsylvania, is just twenty miles away. We agree to get there and find somewhere on the fringes of town to scout for supplies and, hopefully, a house where we can safely spend the night. Harrisburg is a reasonably large city, so we should have no trouble picking up gasoline and food anywhere we want. I'm dying for a cup of coffee; too bad all the roadside convenience stores are closed. Even if they're open, they're *really* open—broken glass, expired food, expired clerks, no fresh coffee. I despise instant coffee, but here at the end of things, it's still better than no coffee. I start to scan the sides of the road for a grocery store.

We slow down by necessity as we reach the western edge of the city, as there are more disabled vehicles scattered hither and yon on the highway. Stopping for a minute to stretch our legs and switch back to me as the driver, we look out to the east to see a glow from the city in the falling light. It hasn't been visible until now, but it's a significant light. It's the light of a living city, brightening the horizon with the combination of street lights, office building lights, and car lights. A living city! We scramble back into the truck as one and hurry onward, closing in on the outskirts of the city as quickly as the debris on the road will allow. Maybe hope is here in southern Pennsylvania.

The highway runs across the northern part of the city and then crosses the Susquehanna River as it wanders north to south. We see nothing as we enter the city and stop on the bridge spanning the river, piling out of the truck and walking to the concrete barrier overlooking the water. Most of the metropolis proper abuts the river to our south.

It's a city in flames. The glow we saw is from a massive fire that's raging across the entire city on the eastern shore of the Susquehanna. The inferno licks at the sky, pouring black clouds into the atmosphere, thankfully being blown away from us by a light breeze sweeping gently from the northwest.

It strikes me that this is what cities in World War II must have looked like. Even from a distance, it's horrible. There has never been anything like this on US soil, at least not since the Civil War and Sherman's sweep of destruction through southern cities. Even then, the scale can't compare. From edge-to-edge of our line of sight, fire consumes everything. We're transfixed by the vision, resting our arms on the cool concrete as the light from the sun dims and the orange embers of a dying Harrisburg brighten.

It roars. I've read news stories about wildfires in the western part of the country over the past few years and descriptions from firefighters about the sound, but nothing compares to the real thing. It's a combination of a jet engine right on top of your head and an unsettling, angry sound beneath as nature eagerly devours all that man has built. As we watch and listen, our hopeful energy dwindles away like the smoke blowing from the ruins.

I notice the sharp cracks of gunfire in the distance. Lots of gunfire—small arms, all to the south and from what seems to be within the area enclosed by flames.

"There must be people there," says DeeDee. "We need to go help them, maybe join them. We've got guns, we could help."

I think about that. We haven't seen anyone alive since Jack—no one on our drive thus far, though I'm sure there are pockets of people gathering and hiding all over the country, fighting back, and, of course, dying at the hands and mouths of the rampaging horde of death. Part of me wants to find more people, but part of me is happy with our small group. With just the few of us, we can manage food, water, transportation, decisions, housing, and so on with limited difficulty. Any group much larger than this will involve complications and inevitable people bullshit.

I know in my head that a part of me—larger than I readily want to admit—is becoming ever more okay with the concept that most of my fellows in the human race have fallen out of the race permanently. We had become a rude culture made up of far too many selfish, "me-first," consumptive, boorish people. It felt like the world was racing toward a something, an undefined something, but we were sprinting to get to it first, to use everything up before the next person could—and to hell with the future and those who came behind. I'm not throwing stones in a glass house, mind you, since I'm far from perfect, but I feel I had always retained one important quality, perhaps the most important: respect. Respect for others, for women, for the world, for myself, for what I do, and for the future. Many of the things on that list were getting crossed off permanently and at a horrifying pace.

I glance skyward, through the vague, white clouds drifting above our heads to mingle with the ebony of the fire's smoke as Harrisburg fights, dies, and burns. My thoughts about God have always been unclear and unsettled. I have a clear sense of the word "faith," but not in terms of some omniscient puppet master, rather in terms of you should believe in what you want to believe, even if it's only a belief in yourself. In my opinion, religion is for each person to define for themselves, though not many people in the history of mankind have agreed with that idea. Exhibit A: millions of people died in myriad wars fought on the globe, most of which were about a difference in beliefs. If there is a God, he or she or it is ripping pissed at us, and maybe we deserve it.

"No," I reply. DeeDee looks at me in surprise. "Think about it, any people down there have come to two conclusions: they're going to die and they're going to take as many of them down as possible before they go. No one sets a whole city on fire if there is any hope of winning." Except maybe Detroit—they seemed to have done that for fun in the old days, which never made any sense. "This is a desperate move by doomed people. All we would do is add to the body count on both sides. I want to get out of here. I want us to live."

I look at the faces of the three women for agreement. All of them look devastated but resigned. A stray tear runs down Eve's cheek as she looks over my shoulder at the orange-red inferno where a city and people are dying with the bravery that only humans seem to muster.

Three heads nod slowly and four sets of feet climb back into the truck without further comment.

We leave the blazing and doomed city behind us as quickly as we can. We're not going to stay here—no one is. The reflection of the flames lingers in the rearview mirror for a long time as the road winds across the river and then edges back north. I hope those who are going to die do so with dignity, and I hope that if God is waiting for them, he has a nice place for them to land since this land is no longer so nice.

***

After what we've seen in the city, we decide that instead of finding a house around here to rest for the night, we'll just continue up the highway for another thirty minutes. Once enough time passes, we just stop in the middle of the road to make the best of it. I take first watch, sitting on top of our supplies in the bed and scanning in all directions. My nap prior to Harrisburg has helped. I have never been a great sleeper—too much going on in my brain despite what was a pretty unremarkable life before—so a few hours are plenty. I listen to the various metal pieces of the truck tick and click as they cool, and the creak and call of the assorted critters out there who don't know, notice, or care that millions of their predators have been swept aside. All the sounds calm me. We're going to at least find peace like this, I hope, in New York.

Hahahaha! Now, there's something that hasn't been said a whole lot.

You're not helping.

Dude, Captain Obvious is now the king of the world. No more prettying up what's said or done—it's time to kill or die. You need me, like it or not.

I hate Captain Obvious sometimes, especially since he's usually right.

But it should be quiet in upstate New York since it's so remote from everything in the best of times. It should also be defensible if needed, and it's a simple place that will maybe let us forget a little bit of whatever it is that needs forgetting. There's no point in joining or starting fights like the one in Harrisburg—the zombies are basically going to win ninety-nine percent of those, so I want to escape in order to protect my people.

I have always been aware that I want to help people as an underlying need, like loose change for a person down on their luck, or bringing them into a convenience store and letting them shop for ten bucks worth of actual food so I can see the money go to a good use instead of smokes or beer. Whenever charitable drives for things at work came up, like donating to food pantries or for school supplies, I was all in. I even tried to do simple stuff like helping co-workers with something they didn't understand or taking some of their work late in the day to lift that burden so they could get home to their families sooner since I'd had none of my own to hurry to.

That desire to help has morphed into a drive to protect the three slumbering girls inside the truck at any cost—this is my new job and responsibility. I feel my hands tighten on the rifle resting across my knees and hear the tentative creak of the wood in the stock from the pressure. We're going to be okay—I will do everything I can to make sure of that.

Me again. Really? What does "okay" look like now? There are tens of thousands, or maybe millions of zombies out there, all of them intent on the simplest things ever—eating and killing. Good luck with "okay."

Luckily, that conversation ends as I feel a shift in the truck. It's DeeDee moving around, opening the door quietly, and shielding the dome light with her other hand so as not to wake Amelie or Eve. She climbs down and out, pushes the door back to the jamb, shoves firmly and carefully to fully shut it, and makes her way along the side of the moonlit truck to clamber up into the truck bed. In her curious way, she immediately snuggles against me and rests her head between my chest and stomach, wrapping her left arm around me as far as possible.

The contrast between her and Eve is striking in this way. DeeDee is completely comfortable with physical contact without reservations and treats me like a giant teddy bear to have and to hold. To her, being close is as natural as breathing, and there is no need to ask whether it's okay or not. Eve, on the other hand, wants physical contact from time to time, but it's only on cautious terms and certainly never with the brazen full-contact approach that DeeDee takes.

Part of me is afraid of what the future holds since it feels like, at some point, there will be a change in the depth of my relationship with one of them, which, of course, will potentially cause my relationship with the other to go in the opposite direction. That's how it would have worked in the past; maybe it's different now, but I'm always mindful that a choice of some kind is going to arrive and probably not too far in the future. To date, I've avoided thinking about this too much, and I force my mind to dance away from the topic yet again. While I've become very fond of both of them, I don't know how they feel about me, nor do I plan on asking.

Like most men since the beginning of time, I foolishly think I'll have any input into that choice. I'm going to be wrong, though, of course, I don't know it yet.

"What are you thinking about?" DeeDee asks, her voice quiet and gentle against my torso.

"Oh, you know, same things us boys have always thought about, mostly nothing and then some about cars and girls," I say it lightly but regret saying it at all as soon as it escapes my mouth.

"Yeah, that sounds about right. I've never wondered much about what y'all were thinking since, for me, it's mostly been pretty obvious. From maybe about age fourteen, all you think about is boobs, girls, and sex. Around sixteen, cars come in. Then around when you hit thirty or so, you add money into that, but I don't think much else," she says with a hint of winsome regret.

Sadly, I think she's awfully damn close to the truth about most of the male population. Jack certainly had not changed his stripes, even after everything. He put his craven desires ahead of morality and the good of the group. I want to change the subject before it goes any further since I'm not sure I'm ready to find out how DeeDee feels.

You're so brave. Two fine-looking gals and you're afraid to even talk to them about anything beyond survival. I'd call you a pussy, but you don't even deserve the word since you're not chasing it even though it's right in front of you. You kiss her, the party's on, or you can just keep living like some prideful, self-righteous monk, "nobly" suffering intentional abstinence.

Just fuck off, you.

"I was actually thinking about the rest of the trip," I say. "We have about a hundred miles until we get to Eve's town and then another hundred and thirty or so after that. We should be able to get to the end of the trip by the end of tomorrow. And then we get something of a fresh start unless there are surprises. I'm kinda nervous that things are different than they were, but at least, in my life, if there was one place that didn't change much, it's there. My grandparents got a little bit older every year, of course, but everything else looked the same or was in its same place as it always was. That was comforting for a kid, and I hope for the grown-ups now too."

DeeDee's quiet for a minute. "I hope for that too," she says. "I've never had a place like that or a regular family, not that this is a normal family exactly, but you know what I mean. My growin' up years were never sitting still. My mom was going through men like a soccer mom changed outfits, and those men mostly weren't good ones." She pauses, likely in recollection of an unpleasant memory. I stop myself from wondering any further what it is. Whatever it is, it's already done and gone, so I can't fix it.

"I hope it's what you hope for. I think we can be happy there, and safe, and together." She punctuates the last word with a squeeze and adds, "Thank you."

We both go silent. I drift in my thoughts some more, hoping she's right and wondering at a woman who has done an amazing job of having her shit together when life has shoveled an awful lot of it at her. I squeeze her back. It doesn't take long for her to settle back into sleep, her breath steadying and her weight resting more heavily against me. It's nice to hold someone, it really is.

CHAPTER 3

I awake with a start to the sound of Eve tapping lightly against the glass of the rear window. The sun is creeping over the horizon in a soothing, purple and pink ribbon at the tops of the trees to the west, and my neck is sore as hell. I'm annoyed with myself for falling asleep, though I'm sure I needed more rest. DeeDee slowly stirs awake too. Looking around quickly to ensure there are no creatures stirring, I confirm there are not. No maids a-milking or swans a-swimming either. Good.

The rest of the morning is spent traveling the rest of the way north toward Lake Ariel. Traffic is light (ha ha), and there's minimal congestion on the road from leftover accidents and abandoned cars, so we make good time. There are no zombies in sight, which is nice and promising, though the realist in me isn't optimistic that, out of dumb luck, Eve's family has survived in their pocket of the country while most everyone else is gone.

We exit the highway at Eve's direction and head east. She has visibly perked up and is feeling chatty. She tells us about how she grew up here, went to college, and then headed south to Charlotte to pursue her career. That's when she met her husband and landed in the neighborhood we used to share. From the way she's acting, her memories are clearly fond ones that remind me of my upbringing—nothing spectacular or notable except to yourself and the attachment we all have to the past in varying degrees. I wonder what Amelie thinks of all this since her late childhood reminiscing, assuming she lives long enough to do so, is going to be cluttered with the mess of the world and the death of everyone she knows. All we can do is hope for a better future for her, for all of us.

After less than thirty minutes, we slowly creep into Eve's town. Amelie's riding in the new "shotgun," her head and torso out of the moonroof as she scans our perimeter in search of critters. The town seems peaceful enough, which, of course, is probably like every town in America at this point. Few cars are askew in the street, and there are no visible corpses of either kind on the main drag. The buildings don't appear to be damaged, though no humans are out and about on errands either.

We continue out the other side of the modest downtown and stop briefly at a convenience store to fill the gas tank and grab some snacks. You know, it's true, Twinkies last forever, or at least through wave one of the apocalypse. I grab my first one in years, along with some beef jerky. We breakfast there in the parking lot, but Eve is clearly impatient to get through the last couple of miles. So we eat quickly and get back in the truck and drive through the meandering roads until she directs me to turn right up ahead.

I stop the truck in disbelief as the street sign comes into view. West Shore Drive. I'm utterly shocked as I turn to look at her in the passenger seat. The street I grew up on during my high school years in New York was West Shore Drive.

"What's wrong?" she queries.

"Is this really your street?" I ask, just dumbfounded.

"Yes, it is," she replies with a confused look on her face. "Why?"

"The road where I grew up, it was … it had the same name." I'm shocked at the coincidence—this is too random that two people grew up in different states on a dinky street with the same name in a small town, then moved to a northern Charlotte suburb, followed by the world getting wiped out by a zombie plague, and then end up together. I glance skyward for a second and wonder if there really *is* something up there. If there is, it has a rather wicked sense of humor.

"Whoa, that's crazy," DeeDee says from the back.

"How can that be? I mean, what are the odds?" Eve sounds just as confused as I am.

"About the same as the Browns winning the Super Bowl at this point. Hell, about the same as they'd been before." Well, no matter. We're here, the world was—and apparently still is—tiny and full of funny collisions.

So I keep moving down the street until I begin to see what may be the lake flickering through gaps in the trees lining the road. Houses line both sides of the road. They sit on generous lots that are well over an acre and filled with old oaks, maples, and evergreens in no particular patterns.

…ddled under the dense
…o-car carports covering
…ckup trucks and sedans—
…vered car here and there. It
…rican town clustered around a
…to settle down and enjoy raising
…e lake or on the green in the center
…especially since there are no creatures
…quirrel or two going about the business
…m to be up to.

…a half-mile of similar homes, Eve sits up
…focuses her attention on a blue-shuttered
…e on our left with a dingy, red Ford pickup and
…own Victoria gathering dust under the carport.
…e being told to stop, I pull into the gravel and grass
…ay and shut off our truck. A few moments pass in
…ce, and then she opens her door and slowly climbs down
…to the yard that runs right to the edge of the crushed
pewter-colored stone of the parking space. I watch her look
around the yard, property, and neighborhood. Neither of
us move, and there's not a sound from DeeDee or Amelie
either. We all get it.

Rather than push Eve to act, I drop out of the truck and,
bringing the pistol and shotgun with me, walk down the
driveway toward the house, the gravel steadily crunching
beneath my running shoes—running shoes are "it" nowadays
since I'm faster than *them*, which is damn helpful sometimes.
I can at least sweep the property and ensure we're alone
and safe from any threat while Eve soaks in memories and

decides what to do. The lawn slopes progressively toward the water as I pass the house on the left side and the backyard. Nothing threatening. There's an old swing strung between a pair of even older oaks, a birdbath gone green with algae resting in the middle of some patio, wrought iron and wood sitting benches. There's a stone path that meanders through the trees and leads all the way down to the water, which I skip as I continue my circle of the house. Coming up from the far side, I face Eve near the corner of the house and just watch her for a moment or two. Her brown hair drifts across her fair skin as she keeps looking at the house, not seeing me or anything else but home.

I walk across the grass to meet her, and she starts a little. "It's been a long time since I've been here. Years. I'm afraid," and I feel little," she says quietly.

I just nod. There's nothing to say. I just need to be here for her and give her whatever she needs.

She takes the first step down the walkway. I follow behind her as she slowly steps onto the brick stoop and hesitates at the door. Bending down to a flower pot full of what looks like dead geraniums drooping over its edges, she lifts it and picks up a silver key from underneath. She fits it to the lock and turns with a click that sounds like a shotgun blast in the heavy silence. I move to enter first, but she pushes past me and swings the blue door open into a dark foyer.

More silence and a stale smell of being closed up. There's another odor I don't recognize. Maybe of older people in an older home, both getting more tired as they age. But there's definitely no reek of zombie. The house, like every other house in the world, is dark without power, the only light coming through gingham curtains in the living room to the left of the entryway. Faded couches and armchairs with white doilies at the headrests occupy the floor, and assorted family photos line a chair rail encircling the room. We walk slowly into the kitchen, which is decorated in classic country—brown table, blue tablecloth, brown chairs, brown cabinets, and a wooden floor. A hallway leads off to the right. That must be where all the bedrooms are. I hear Eve begin to make her way down in that direction. I walk to the kitchen sink and look out at a beautiful view of the lawn. The lake shimmers as it laps the shoreline. I'm lost in the view of the water, thinking ahead to the lake at my grandparents' cabin and what awaits us there other than my own memories, when I hear Eve shriek.

The sound snaps me out of my reverie, and I tear down the hallway with the pistol at the ready, sure that she's being savaged by a zombie or something else and furious with myself for not clearing the house before allowing her to walk off alone. Although, the locked front door tickles my brain and slows my passage as I near the final door on the left. I hear her sobbing from within the room.

"Daddy!" she cries as I enter. She's hunkered down aside a brass-framed bed in between two windows overlooking the back yard and lake. The smell I hadn't recognized earlier strikes me full blast, wafting over me in a sour wave—it's the smell of critical sickness and a foul bed. There's a shrunken man beneath a thick comforter on the bed. His skin is wrinkled, thin, and is a terrible grayish color that hints at deep illness and being closer to the end than the beginning. He's dying, and his time is short. A living human, but not for long from what I can tell. Her father. Murky eyes flick in my direction as I stop in the doorway, then back to Eve.

There's noise back toward the front of the house as DeeDee and Amelie come bursting through the door in response to Eve's cry. I motion them to be silent and signal that all is okay, or at least safe, and they stop in the space between the kitchen and hallway. Leaving Eve, I back out of the sickroom and usher them outdoors, explaining what I know and settling us down onto the grass out front in the afternoon sun. How horrible—hoping to find your family for months, that connection to the past, to those who cared for you, only to find one of them at the natural end. I ache for Eve and see the same on the faces of the other two. I also think forward and hope this isn't my fate too. Rather than sit there helplessly, I go to the truck and break out some food to keep us occupied while Eve remains inside. We pick at the food listlessly, drink from our supply of bottled water, and wait.

An hour passes before Eve comes to the door, her tear-streaked face all puffy and red. She waits for a minute and then comes down to join us. She sits next to DeeDee and leans into her arms for comfort. All of us keep quiet.

"He's dying, dammit," she says suddenly. "He thinks it's cancer but knows it doesn't matter what it is, just that it's terminal. He lived through the fucking zombies, through losing Mom as they all fought back, only to have this … this … *thing* find him."

I don't know what to say. What is there to say? Everyone has been thrown a shitty curveball, but this is an extra one, and it sounds like that man is going to die no matter what we do. DeeDee rubs Eve's back, soothing her as much as possible.

She continues. "He's been sick for a few months, unable to do much more in the last couple of weeks than drink some water from time to time. A healthy, tough, sixty-year-old man reduced to lying alone in a bed in an empty house in an empty town and waiting to die. They fought the zombies when they came, everyone died, including my mother, but they killed a bunch of them and things quieted down. He made do through the winter and was going to come to North Carolina to look for me when it first hit him, terrible weakness and vertigo, loss of appetite, and then just this … he can barely move and when he does, it's pure agony.

"He told me they're back, too, more zombies and a lot of them from what he could tell. They've been up and down the street a few times. It sounds like they're patrolling, like they did back in North Carolina, but he thinks they either don't smell him because he's sick or are avoiding him *because* he's sick."

Super. A dying man who we can't move and probably can't leave behind, and a town full of zombies. Anyone want to kick me in the nuts with steel-toed boots while we're at it?

***

We spend the next couple of hours going through neighboring houses for more supplies because you just can't ever have enough. We're here and the residents are zombie luncheon meat. I go in and sweep the house first and then stand guard while Amelie and DeeDee collect whatever's useful. Eve won't budge from her house, and there's no sense in trying to change her mind.

More soup, more water, though clearly the folks of Lake Ariel are not huge bottled-water drinkers. Fine by me. When bottled water cost more per gallon than gasoline, it seemed a bit ridiculous to me. Plus, our population had gotten carried away with the habit of buying bottled water, and it troubles me to think of all the empty bottles in landfills because so many were too lazy to recycle them. Not a problem anymore. Americans had been slipping, but I also admit I had maybe a couple more soapboxes than your average bear.

One nice find: a pair of hunting bows and a huge assortment of arrows. One of them is a crossbow, a nasty-looking little weapon, and the other is a camouflaged compound bow I can draw but not for long. Seems like I'm due for a little more shoulder, chest, and arm exercise. I don't think they'll kill a zombie unless it's a perfect head shot, but they may at least come in handy if we need to do any quiet hunting for food. Another shotgun and several boxes of shells go into the bed of the truck too. Who would have thought that the twenty-first century would bring an urgent need for as many weapons as you can haul instead of the newest smartphone?

As the day winds down, DeeDee and I walk up and down West Shore Drive from end to end, enjoying the clear air but also watching out for anything moving in our temporary neighborhood. Amelie is resting in the truck bed, standing watch with the rifle at the ready so Eve is free to be with her father. We're going to have to spend the night here, which I hope is going to be a peaceful one, though we'll rotate watches and be ready. I'm not thrilled with the house in terms of defensibility because I don't know the area at all or how many zombies are around, but the windows are small, the lines of sight are decent, and a fat moon is already on the low horizon, so I'll have its ghostly light, at least.

"What are we going to do?" DeeDee asks as she scans her side of the road.

"What do you mean?"

"You know what I mean," she replies. "Eve isn't going to leave her daddy, not with him dying and all, and we can't stay here, I don't think."

No, we can't, and I don't want to, even if we can. Too close to other towns, which means there will be more of them to deal with, and probably not cold enough in the winter to give us a break as the cold either slows down or freezes the zombies to re-death. Not that winter is going to be much fun for us either up in New York. The cabins only have baseboard heaters, and it isn't like the power is switched on anyway, but it seems like a fair tradeoff to have some peace through the winter. There's a fireplace in the main cabin we can keep running around the clock at least, assuming the smoke or smell won't draw anyone, or anything, to us.

"I guess we'll either have to stay here until he dies and then keep going, or somehow try to convince Eve to leave him and come with us. But I don't think we can stay here for long."

She looks at me as if I'm an utter moron. "Would you leave your father as he was dying? Even in this mess?" She eyes me like a third eye is about to sprout from the middle of my forehead. Whoops. One of those times where I'm only (and barely) thinking with my head.

"No," I answer, "I guess I was thinking only about the good of the group instead of her feelings. I want us all to stay together so we can be as safe as possible, but you're right. I'd never leave if it was my parents. I was thinking more about the destination than the journey. I've been like that forever, so I guess I was just dead set on getting to New York."

Ah, the destination, the old "finish what you started" thing you've done your whole life. Like finishing the round of golf after you saved and then killed the possibly-infected woman. You should leave now and make Eve come with you. Fact: he is going to die. Fact: you don't want to lose part of your new family. Fact: if you force her to come with you, you're going to fuck up your new family. Fact: this is a nice little pickle. Maybe he dies fast. Maybe you can help that along ....

We finish patrolling in silence as the shadows grow long and the air turns crisper. I'm deep in thought about what to do and how to solve this new problem. Do I need to solve it myself, or should I let life happen the way it's going to? I don't have an answer; I hate not having the answers.

***

Later that evening, we settle for sleep, with DeeDee in one
of the bedrooms, Amelie on the couch, and Eve curled up
in a tattered, once-gold, wingback chair she asked me to
move from the den into the sickroom. I take watch, and
after a little while indoors, I decide it will be better to be
outside so I'll have both a line of sight and hearing. We
have not brought much in the way of heavy clothes with us
from North Carolina and the air is sharp as I step onto the
back deck, so I silently retreat into the house to find a coat
closet. Finding one near the front door, I dig out a heavy,
sheepskin-lined, flannel jacket that smells of pipe smoke
and the outdoors. It must belong to Eve's father. As I slip
it on, I realize he was indeed a big and healthy man since it
fits me fine with a little room to spare. How he turned into
that shrunken thing dying in the back room, I don't know.

Back outside, I look up at the moon, able to make out
every detail of its pockmarked surface as it hovers above
the otherwise pitch-black town. That's a remarkable part
of the new world—it's dark, dark, dark, and the skies are
clearer than they have ever been. Before, there was always
some kind of ambient light from something somewhere on
the horizon, not to mention streetlights, house lights, and
the ever-present headlights from cars full of people going
somewhere all the time. Now, the world is enveloped in a
black cloak each evening, and the only sounds are courtesy
of Mother Nature. Unless, of course, zombies are on the
prowl. Then it isn't quiet nor peaceful, especially back at the
beginning of the end when the screams of the dying in the

night shattered any chance of rest until most everyone was dead. Then it was the nightmares that ruined sleep.

I settle into a weathered Adirondack chair facing the monochrome lake and let myself relax into the silence of my own as I open my ears for anything moving. I'll circle the house every hour or so, but I'm sure I'll pick up any disturbance from this vantage point. No problem staying awake since I have yet to figure out what we should do next, and it's certainly cold enough to keep me sharp.

DeeDee asked me to wake her so she could have a turn at being the lookout, and while I told her I would, I'm going to let her sleep. This is good for me—it's peaceful here, and I picture doing virtually the same thing in New York, sitting on the porch of my grandparents' cabin, looking over a lake, relaxing, and feeling safe. I crave peace. My entire life has been busier than I think I've wanted, though that realization only came when the world went silent and the initial horror wound down. Silence is soothing, I'm completely comfortable with it, and never mind the solitude of quiet time. This is what I seek for us: quiet, peace, and sanctuary. I feel an obligation to provide those things for the three women despite the current problem.

No one wears a watch anymore, so it's just a guess as to how much time passes before I hear the soft creak of the door opening behind me. Maybe an hour or more, not that it matters. I know who it's going to be. I figured she would come eventually.

"Can't sleep?" I ask.

"Could you if you were me?"

CHAPTER 4

Morning brings a cloudy day to match the jumble of my thoughts. We're only a few hours from the cabin, but it feels like an incomplete trip now that Eve has decided to stay behind. DeeDee was upset when she woke up and I explained the nighttime conversation, both at me for standing watch all night and then more so that Eve is leaving the group, though she too understood. Without a father in her life, or really anything remotely resembling a normal family, DeeDee seems the most in tune with the concept of togetherness now and fights to keep the tears from her eyes. Amelie has bonded more closely to DeeDee than Eve, so while she was also out of sorts by Eve's decision, it didn't appear to impact her too terribly. I spent time in the morning trying to change Eve's mind, or seeing if there was a way to bring her father with us for the relatively short drive, but neither budged. Moving the now-ancient man even a fraction brought him severe pain and bubbling blood to his lips.

Since they're going to be effectively housebound until he dies, we're leaving a good portion of our food supplies behind for them along with one of the shotguns, a pistol, and a ton of ammunition. He isn't going to eat any of the food, and I desperately hope she won't need the weapons, but if there's anything you can be sure of now, it's that life is not a box of chocolates.

I ensure that the truck in the carport will start and run, and I top the fuel tank off from our jerry cans since we can stop for more of everything on the rest of the trip. There are maps of Pennsylvania and New York in the glove box of her family's Crown Vic, so I draw out directions for Eve from her house to where we're going to be, hoping that we'll make it there, he'll die quickly, and she will be able (and inclined) to join us. I have never travelled to the cabins from this direction, always coming from the southeast, but it will be easy enough for her to follow.

Amelie and DeeDee say their goodbyes—Amelie standing somewhat awkwardly in the driveway and crying softly until Eve goes to her and gives her a hug, whispering something in her ear as they break. The poor kid has been through so much already, and surely the situation here isn't easy for her as she may be thinking about her parents on top of the segregation of our little family. DeeDee is still visibly miserable, her eyes red and chin trembling gently, but she gives Eve a long, fierce embrace and hard kiss on the cheek. I stand like "that kid" at a high school dance, without a date and without any confidence, hoping someone will come talk to me but trying to look like I'm not bothered that nobody does. While the women are still milling around near our truck, I go back into the house and make my way through the sickening air, down the hallway, and to the threshold of the bedroom that houses Eve's father. If it's possible, he looks even worse just this one day later, sunken eyes meeting mine and frail fingers gesturing me to the wing chair at his bedside.

I try not to breathe too deeply, as his inability to get out of the bed has fouled both the bed and the air in the room. I really, really want to open some of the windows in the room to air it out, thinking Eve should not have to contend with the horribly failing body of her father in this way, but I don't. Despite being buried in several layers of blankets, he's shivering. I realize that along with his physical suffering, it has to be terrible to surrender his dignity as well.

You can kill two birds with one stone, you know. Put him out of his misery, keep the band together, finish the tour. One pillow, probably less than one minute, and he's gone. Not like he can fight you, and no one but you and me would ever know a thing.

It's an obvious solution, and while the me of a year ago would never have considered it, the me in charge of keeping all of us alive is inclined to listen to the never-ending Voice of Truth. Without being conscious of doing so, I lean forward over the bed.

"You're leaving," comes the croak from the bed.

I'm startled and abruptly sit back in the chair. I had not heard a sound from him before and didn't expect it. "Yes, we are. This place isn't safe for all of us, so I'm taking the other two with me now, and Eve is hopefully going to follow after, after …" Now that it's coming out of my mouth, talking about his death seems far more personal than practical. Especially for him.

"After I die, you mean," he rasps sharply.

"She won't leave you, even though I admit I tried to get her to."

He sighs slowly. "I don't want her to leave. I don't want to die alone, here in this house. I need her here with me." He breaks eye contact with me as he speaks, and I see a single tear slither from his left eye and meander sideways in the crow's foot astride his eye before dripping heavily onto the bedspread.

"I get it, but I don't get it. You're going to die soon, and keeping her here is probably a death sentence for her, too, and you know it, you selfish bastard." I'm mad now. It's bad enough that she feels the responsibility to stay here and help him die as peacefully as possible, but it's a whole other thing to hear that he has probably guilted her into doing so.

Do it. Just do it. No one will ever know, except me. And it's not like I swing through and remind you of your shortcomings or failures or anything. It'll be fine, trust me, go ahead.

I try to control my breathing and settle down. I'm not going to kill this man; time and his sickness are going to take care of that soon enough. All I can do is ensure Eve can come to us when that happens. I can also come back for her in a couple of weeks once we're settled and safe in New York. There's a risk that we'll miss each other, but since there's only the route I've given her between here and there and not exactly a lot of traffic on the roads, I'll see her if we happen to be on the road at the same time. Yeah, that's good enough.

"Die fast. Let her go. Both." I stand and look down into his eyes that glare back at me with the anger of a strong man trapped in a weak body. I leave the room without looking back and go out into the front yard. I wrap Eve in my arms tightly, smelling her hair as it brushes my nose, and realize that this is the first time I've felt this side of her body against mine since she's always slept back-to-back with me. Stepping back, I hold her shoulders at arm's length and look at her, trying to burn this moment in my mind and hoping this is not the last I'll see of her.

"Be careful. You know they're out there, so don't take any chances. We'll be there, waiting for you when it's time. You know how to find us," I tell her. I don't know what else to say, so I turn and join DeeDee and Amelie in the truck.

All of the windows are down as the women wave farewell and call to Eve.

As if on cue, from far, far in the distance, like the sound of a lonely wolf calling for whatever it is wolves call for: *Muuuuuuuhhhhh!*

CHAPTER 5

I divide my attention between the road and the rearview mirror as we drive away, half afraid that a horde of zombies has been lurking in the tree line, waiting until we leave, and are about to swarm like bees to honey to grab Eve, but nothing happens other than her slight form shrinking in the distance. A turn in the road takes her completely out of sight. I'm not happy, really torn between staying for however long it takes for the old man to die and continuing the journey and protecting Amelie and DeeDee, but I realize that the group has to come before the individual. Eve is an adult, that's her father, and she gets to make her own choices, though I desperately hope he dies quickly so she can follow us if she chooses to do so.

There's a deep sadness inside her. It was there even before we brought her home, something that seems like it has been years in the making and not a new thing brought on by the end of the world—since, of course, that wasn't enough to make the survivors a smidge droopy ... no, not at all. During our initial time together, when it was just the two of us, I always had a sense she was unhappy with how her life had shaken out, or maybe about the choices she'd made. Eve would talk about her past, but only at a fairly superficial level that made it clear she'd set boundaries around herself for protection. No details about how she really felt about her marriage and divorce. The most she'd ever explained was about the ill-fated New Year's Eve party where she was accosted by Jack. Something just strikes me as her being a little bit broken, and, not surprisingly, I want to fix whatever it is. I worry that she will just stay once he dies and let herself go. I resolve then and there that once we get to New York, get settled and safe, I (or we) will come back here as soon as possible.

Making our way back through the town, we head out to the highway, follow the entrance ramp for northbound traffic, and drive on in silence. DeeDee is pensively watching the countryside roll by through the window, and Amelie sprawls across the broad backseat of the truck, deeply asleep like all young people easily manage to do somehow. The rest of northern Pennsylvania is peaceful and dead quiet, and it isn't long before we hit the border and the "Welcome to New York" sign. The Empire State, once mighty and arguably home to the most important city in the world, now brought to its knees in a virtual blink of an eye. I picture what the City must have been like at the end—lots of people means lots of zombies, and the carnage must have been horrifying and rapid. This is why we seek the much quieter northern section; no sense staying in the southern, heavily-populated areas and inevitably running into more former bankers-turned-flesh-eating-monsters than we can handle. Of course, some of the folks on Main Street would have said this is either no different to how the bankers were before or exactly what they deserve. I have no opinion on that one since it's now in the past and none of it matters. All of the money in the world is now worthless, as are all of the BMWs, boats, vacation homes, giant televisions, and so on. Guns, food, and water, that's the new wealth.

Anticipation rises in my stomach and dances around like a fast food hamburger and fries after a night of heavy drinking. We're less than an hour from the lake, and while I'm hopeful that we will find some of my family there, I'm also practical and trying not to put much stock in the idea. We leave the highway in Oneonta, and Amelie calls for a pit stop to do the roadside necessaries as we enter one of the innumerable small areas off the major thoroughfares that dot the landscape, providing gas, food, and so on. I pull into a strip mall parking lot that houses a handful of stores. It's across the street from one of the independent grocery stores that had stubbornly clung to existence as the wave of big-box stores swept the country before the zombie wave took care of business.

As I climb out of the truck and stroll up the street to give the women some privacy, I come to a store that may prove helpful. Dark windows provide no view of the contents since the sun is behind the building and the sidewalk that stretches in front of the half-dozen connected stores is covered by the overhang of the roof for those rainy days. I briefly wonder just how many of these little strip stores dot the country, all of similar design and vintage. The yellow sign with bright red lettering over the heavy, steel-plated door states, "Eller's Emergency Supplies—Are You Really Ready For Anything?" Now this may be a very worthwhile shopping trip. It's going to be terribly cold in the winter, even inside the cabins, so some warmer clothes, sleeping bags, blankets, and whatever else will be very helpful, and this seems like just the ticket. I certainly haven't been ready for *anything*, just extremely lucky and resourceful so far.

I walk back to the truck to retrieve a flashlight and something bigger than the pistol. The women are done watering the plants and follow me back to the door of the shop, armed and ready, though there's nothing in sight and no sounds.

Not surprisingly, the door drifts open at my touch, allowing the outside sunlight to weakly illuminate the threshold and the contents of the shop that are closest to the door. At first, I flick the flashlight on as I walk in, splashing the light around the depths of the store, but after seeing the first mannequin against the wall, shrouded in camouflaged combat fatigues and a gas mask that makes me jump out of my skin, I walk back to the front window, flip the shotgun around, and rap the butt of the stock sharply against the glass. Nothing happens, but I want more light, so I give it a second go with a good bit more force. Still nothing. Then it hits me. Being "ready" means having safety or bulletproof glass so that whatever you need to be ready for can't come steal your stuff. Duh. You'd think my trip to the demolition store in Charlotte would have taught me that the people who owned stores like this were going to protect them rather enthusiastically. I rummage around the shelves, figuring that camping supplies will be included here, and come across lanterns you wind by hand to generate light. I crank several of them up and place them around the store.

Wonderful. This is the Home Depot of apocalypse-planning. Heavy-duty sleeping bags, weatherproof coats of all sizes, waterproof matches, boots, lanterns, flares, dehydrated food, seed canisters, water jugs, knives of all shapes and sizes—though I'm content with my KNIFE—bug out kits for the car that hold a few days' worth of supplies, long guns locked vertically along one wall in a display case, ammo in glass-topped cabinets. You name it, it's all there—with the exception of explosives. You can't have enough of all this stuff, and we're going to take as much of it as we can, especially since we left a good bit of food behind with Eve.

Leaving Amelie and DeeDee in the store, I walk back out into the parking lot and back the truck up to the front door so we can load up. We grab four of the sleeping bags in case Eve makes it, lots of the dehydrated food, wool blankets, coats, hats, gloves, boots, and just about one of everything else we think will be useful. I love the lanterns since it's damn dark at the lake in the best of times and, without power, it's going to be gloomy in the evenings, especially in winter with the shorter days. There's also a small supply of slow-burning candles that we grab and some canteens we can use for the spring-fed well just inside the property line on the path that encircles the lake. I'm not able to find the key to the locking cable through the rifles and shotguns, but we have our current assortment, and I know there are three or four more waiting for us at the lake, so I'm not put off by that. Ammo, however, I add to our supply after smashing the cabinets open—Whew! After the front window failure, I was worried it was just me getting older and weaker—and grab every box that matches our weapons. The truck is big and already well-loaded, but we now have a miniature mountain tied down under a desert camo tarp in the bed. We collect the lit lanterns on our way out, and I turn before exiting to say a silent thanks to Eller for being so prepared. I picture a guy sitting on the front porch of a cabin, surrounded by weapons and infrared scopes. He's snacking on beef jerky, reading a book, and waiting for them to come. If that's true, I wish him good fortune. Or maybe it's a "her" … you never know.

The roadway is largely clear as we travel east on Route 23, the only exception being a nasty collision between an 18-wheeler and farm tractor with a trailer that we have to go well off the paved surface to circumnavigate. The huge, rolled, six-foot-tall straw bales from the tractor's trailer had exploded and littered the road and shoulders. I wonder how fast the semi had been going when they had their unfortunate meeting.

It takes me a few minutes to notice, but it occurs to me that I'm driving more slowly the closer we get, and I clear my head to get the driving portion of the journey over and done. The access road that leads up to the couple of dozen houses encircling the lake community—well, "community" may be a stretch; these are predominantly tiny, summer-type cottages strewn around a correspondingly tiny lake at the outskirts of a really tiny town to begin with—comes into vision on the right. I slow the truck to make the turn onto the bone dry dirt and scree surface that sharply heads uphill.

Memories of going up this hill, fishtailing and spraying loose gravel in every direction in an overpowered (for the time) '80s muscle car, come back. It isn't going to be the last flash from the past that reaches out for me. I know that, but the clarity with which it comes to mind is a bit surprising.

The lake was always something of a mental mystery to me as I achieved adulthood. Visits here were only annual from when I was in diapers to shortly after I entered high school, and even then, it was mostly only for the holiday weekends that bracketed the summer months. Despite that, of my childhood memories, most of the clearest ones are of this place. Perhaps that's because the trips were always highly anticipated in addition to the short duration, so my brain must have clamped on to those days with the temerity of a zombie eating a fat kid. Also, while my childhood had been a steady series of changes like anyone else, the lake barely changed. My grandparents got incrementally older from year to year, but not so much that an eight- or twelve-year-old would notice. However, everything else was always the same, and that was part of what I looked forward to each time. The fond memory of this board game, that rock with a fossil embedded in it, the funny signs along the driveway, the books, the blueberry bushes, and so on was reinforced by being the same every single time. Now, we'll see what has happened since my last visit.

"Are we there yet?" DeeDee pipes up beside me. "Hey, are you in there?"

I shake myself loose of the past, not realizing I've come to a complete stop at the base of the hill, and grin at her as I press the gas pedal down. "Yeah, sorry. Memory lane there for a minute. Think that's going to happen to me a lot coming up. It's been a long time since I've been here."

We drive up the hill, listening to the familiar rumble of gravel beneath the tires as we come near the split in the road where the sides open up onto sprawling corn fields on either side of the road. Taking the right fork, I quickly come to the driveway carved like a tunnel from the birches lining the road. I start to turn in when DeeDee shouts at me, "Stop! You can't go in there!"

Ha. I'm so used to it I don't even really notice the sign wired to the open gate at the end of the driveway. It's a One Way sign, with the arrow pointing out. Like many before her, DeeDee has been thrown by the sign, which didn't mean a thing other than the fact that my grandfather had a mischievous sense of humor. Apprehension races around my insides.

"Um, it's okay. I'm pretty sure no one is coming out," I chuckle and swing into the cool, heavily shaded drive. It's dark enough that the automatic headlights of the truck flicker on to light the way. Deadfalls are scattered along the sides of the road that winds through dense fern growth under the birches. Rays of sunlight find their way through the light green overhead foliage onto the crushed stone tire paths and mossy middle patch of greenery that never seems to grow.

More evidence of a clever family with a good sense of humor are nailed to trees as we progress: signs for speed limit 35—if you would like to remove the undercarriage of your car, go right ahead and try for 35; 10 is more like the max—railroad crossing, raise your snowplow, ice cream ahead, and so on. All the signs are, as signs in the countryside always are, inevitably peppered with bullet holes of varying calibers. They've been there for as long as I can recall.

We slowly snake our way through the woods for more than half a mile before finally beginning to descend toward the level of the lake and the cabins. I'm able to glimpse the shimmering surface of the lake reflecting the late afternoon sunlight here and there. Then we're there, at the upper parking area paved in the shards of pine needles above the cabins my family has owned since the early 1900s. There are nearly four hundred acres in the plot, though I suppose, in all likelihood, we now own everything in every direction.

I hesitate again. Some of the childhood excitement of visiting here wafts up to the surface of my consciousness and mixes with anxiety of what if some of my family is here, and if so, are they alive or not, and if not, can I handle that? This was my favorite place to visit as I was growing up. I have been holding on to that tender set of recollections for decades. The hope that some of my family members are here has been foremost in my mind since the moment I decided to make the trip, and I desperately fear there's going to be something coming that is about to destroy one or all of these things.

"It's going to be okay, it is. We're all together, and we'll make anything work," DeeDee says. She is a little wrong since Eve isn't with us, but I know she means well. I have not shared the fine details of how I feel about this place, nor will it hit home for her in the same manner anyway since these are *my* memories, but as always, her heart is in the right place.

I take my foot off the brake pedal and ease onto the last stretch of the driveway as it drops down to the level of the shoreline. We pass the basketball court on the right, though it's not so much a court per se, but rather an open, grassy area with a hoops backboard and goal nailed to two perfectly straight tree trunks. Try dribbling a basketball on grass—piece of cake if you're three-feet tall, but a pain in the ass for a full-height kid or grownup. There were a lot of games of H-O-R-S-E, but not many actual basketball games.

The boathouse comes quickly into view first, with one of the white canoes resting open-side-down on the left side and the paddles stored vertically on brackets screwed to the outside wall of the building. I coast the truck to a stop right next to the outhouse—yes, an actual outdoor crapper, and possibly the most important building on the property going forward—and burn barrel and switch off the ignition. Out of age-old habit, I glance toward the porch of the main cabin to see if my grandparents are coming out to greet us. They're gone, of course, not from the zombies, but from Time's relentless, onward pace. No one appears.

There are no cars in sight either, which means no humans and no family hiding here, safe and sound. I was expecting that, but the reality of it in front of me snuffs out the little flicker of hope I was carrying with me.

In front of the truck is the two-car garage with a workshop space. The doors to the garage aren't powered, but rather they slide side-to-side on large wheels mounted on rails above the doors. I wonder about my grandfather's cars—he had two BMWs, older ones, and once he passed, I lost mental track of them.

Clear memories of sitting in the back seat of the 2800 CS flash through my mind. I remember feeling the leatherette cross-patterned seat below my legs and sliding around on the bench seat as my grandfather drove entirely too fast—according to my grandmother, though it was terribly thrilling to me—on the small town roads. I hope that car is still here, even if it isn't running, which it likely isn't unless someone has been able to maintain it over many years. I just want the chance to sit in the driver's seat for once and take in the familiar scents of gas, oil, old car, and the past. That would make me so happy.

"Are we getting out or not?" DeeDee says, keeping it real and snapping me back to the present.

"Yes, it's just that memories are strong here." Jeez, that sounds like Yoda. Ooooh, a lightsaber! Now that'd be a top-notch zombie-killing tool.

"I get it. This looks like a great place to have come to visit, especially with family …" She trails off, and I recall that her upbringing was less than ideal. I can't change the past, but I plan to do everything I can to ensure that the present and future are as good for her as possible.

"It was, for sure, and now it's ours, our weird little family's place." Amelie titters at this from the back seat, having finally awakened, a hilarious sleep line from the upholstery running from her eyebrow down to her jawline. "That being said, let's check around carefully before we begin to unpack," I say.

We haven't seen any zombies since leaving Eve, which I take as a good sign, but it's also pragmatic enough for me to know that this part of the country could not possibly have escaped unscathed. Despite knowing that, I fervently hope this particular area had, but, if not, that no zombies remain. There are very few residents of the town, with a good chance that farm animals outnumber humans even in this day and age, so my guess is that, whenever the zombies came through, they did what zombies do and then moved along.

"Let's unpack!" Amelie says, like every young person in the history of road trips. "I'm tired of being in the truck."

"Well, before we do that, we have to scout, just to be safe. I'd hate for us to unload everything from the truck and find out we have to leave in a hurry and lose our supplies."

We climb out of the truck and arm ourselves accordingly. Amelie has the rifle and one of the .45s that are as important as clean underwear. DeeDee has the crossbow and a Glock pistol we found in Eve's old neighborhood. As for me, I've got the shotgun with alternating rounds of buckshot and slugs, a .45, and the KNIFE. It's completely silent in the recessed area that the cabins rest in at the bottom of the sloping ground; the only exception is a single chipmunk skittering atop the woodpile—fully stocked, I note, which is very good—and watching the invaders of his kingdom. I scan the immediate area and see that, from the outside, everything is as I remember. The beanbag board painted like a Princeton Tiger's face hangs against an outside wall of the main cabin, the dozen or so kerosene lanterns swing from their usual hooks at the upper frame of the porch, the mixture of chairs are as they always are, and the hammock stretches between two of the pine trees between the cabin and garage. A place for everything, and everything in its place, as comforting as it has always been.

Leading the way, I walk over to the boathouse and find it locked. I don't want to have to break the windows since, when the weather fully turns, we will need every ounce of insulation we can get. So I move over to the garage, but find it locked as well. Not great. I know that one of the year-round residents who lived at the bottom of the hill kept an eye on the place when no one was around and I think I know which house was his, but I don't want to have to go back and then rummage through his house for a key. There has to be one hidden here somewhere for just this reason, though every time I'd come, my grandparents were already here so there was no need.

Wait … that isn't true. I stored an old Chevy II up here over the course of one winter because my folks hadn't the garage space downstate. I had inherited it from a family member, but I didn't have the resources to immediately restore it at the time. My father and I dropped it off and then collected it in the spring. Of course, spring behaves differently here, and we got snarled in six inches of snow on the trip to pick it up. Although, we managed well enough despite some excitement on the curvier hills due to ancient drum brakes on the passenger rear wheel with a tendency to lock without warning.

I let my thoughts relax in order to find details of that trip from ages ago in my head. We did not bring a key on that trip, of that I'm certain, and the garage was definitely locked then too. Well, no use overthinking it since it seems it'll never come to me that way, so I keep going on toward the main cabin. Also locked; the front storm door, the door from the single bedroom onto the porch, and the rear door to the kitchen. The cat door, however, is wide open, but not helpful unless we have some time to train the chipmunk. No better luck with the second or third cabins either.

"Cabin" is an important definition. All of them are stained the same dark brown, with wood siding and green trim. Always had been, and now always will be unless I get really, really bored. The boathouse is made up of two rooms set perpendicular to one another, though the entry room is just that, an entry space that can't be used for anything larger than coat hangers and knick-knack storage like a wooden wagon and the whiffle ball supplies, while the second is used for extra sleeping quarters if needed. The main cabin has a green-painted porch spanning its width and overlooking the small lake. Inside, there's a dining area to your left, adjacent to a living room with fireplace in the middle of the house, and a small sitting area to the right side of the front door. A kitchen shaped like an upside down "L" can be seen as you enter and pass through the dining space, and then there's a full (though compact) bathroom and a very small bedroom that tucks off the den to the right. Beadboard paneling and ceilings arch to meet cathedral-style at the peak of the roof, and the total size is in the neighborhood of six hundred to seven hundred square feet.

The two secondary cabins are also very modest: the closest to the house encompasses a porch upon the lake as well, a pair of bedrooms, and a half bath concealed by a pocket door. Maybe two hundred fifty square feet. The farthest contains a single bedroom and half bath, also with a porch, and is perhaps two hundred square feet. All in, the house I occupied in the Huntersville subdivision was larger than all the buildings combined, but the property adjoining the lake sprawls across roughly four acres of open spaces and buildings, as compared to the token quarter of an acre or less allotted to modern subdivision homes. The separation between each of the buildings spans approximately fifty feet of stubborn grass, blueberry bushes, rhododendrons, and fern-filled natural areas.

Collectively, however, it feels like a miniature estate, especially to a child who could spend an entire day within sight of the buildings and never run out of things to explore and discover.

So, anyway, no key, either visible or in my head. The scouting will have to come first, and we may as well sweep the circuit of the path around the lake. Perhaps I'll get the key to come to mind as we walk, or come up with another way into the house that I won't have to go to a ton of effort to undo.

The path around the lake was two things growing up: a traditional walk for the entire family following lunch, and a course to adventure for me and my sister. Morgan is three years older than me, a tremendous athlete who starred at a Division I volleyball program. She's beautiful, brilliant, and outrageously wild. She was the center of my world growing up; I watched her excel at everything she put her hand to and yet never understood how or why she resisted the pull of brilliance she could have attained by making impulsive and typically poor choices along the way. Grades were never a problem, unless she simply wasn't interested at the time, mastery of sports took no time at all, and boys practically lined up at the curb to court her. Everything came easily for her, except common sense.

There was always a different party to go to, and no, our parents didn't need to know we were going somewhere other than where we'd told them we would be. She would vanish for weekends at a time as an older teen and we would have no clue as to her whereabouts. I was alternatingly fascinated and frightened since the adventures she'd recount to me were like something out of a movie, and the knock-down, drag-out fights she'd have with our parents made me cringe in my room as they thundered at one another. As I got older, I wanted to both protect and save her, but she was bent on her path and nothing was going to sway her.

By the time she (somehow) finished college, my parents were at their wit's end and told her she was on her own, something that Morgan gladly accepted as she swept out the door with a handful of duffle bags to a waiting van full of her friends who were headed for Colorado. She wanted a life full of outdoor adventure and found it there, happily working as a ski instructor—since, of course, picking up skiing was a piece of cake for her—during the winter months, a golf pro (yup, that too, dammit) in the more cooperative weather, and then at just some odd jobs whenever needed in between. Never married, never serious with men beyond brief and explosive relationships as they inevitably tried to tame the wildness and failed. She always sent them off with their tail betwixt their legs.

Morgan was simply the sun—you wanted to look, you couldn't, and you would be absolutely burned for getting too close. I'm the lone exception, as she was like a mother bear protecting me as we grew up. Pity the girl who broke my heart in a stinging teenage romance, as she got an earful that would make an army drill sergeant proud, and if it was one of *those days*, perhaps a bit of physical intimidation for good measure. Wonderful, maddening, incredible Morgan.

We both loved it here, spending all day, every day in motion. The path around the lake led to a handful of diversions: the whiffle ball field, the sprawling growth of blueberry bushes mingled among raspberry and blackberry patches, and the shooting range—which we're going to make use of if all is quiet up here. Not to mention it also hosted the hundreds of foot races we had to see which of us was faster. That was never a mystery though. She won all of those, even as I grew bigger and stronger. She just seemed to float above the ground like all astonishing natural athletes. Even though I was a good athlete of no small accomplishment, I just couldn't keep up with her. She would be waiting back at the porch, seemingly barely winded, as I emerged from the last stretch of woods, dripping with sweat and frustration from another loss, and then we'd go for a swim in the sharply crisp water of the lake to cool down.

Her hair color varied over the years as her whims struck her, but the natural color was dark brown, and she always wore it long down her back. She had shockingly blue eyes that watched people very directly, without fear or self-consciousness—except in whoever was being examined. Arched eyebrows seemed to raise a constant, unspoken question, and her cheekbones rose high to give her something of an aristocratic look. For the rare times she wore makeup, she was a stunning beauty that brought conversation in a room to halt when she entered. Carrying the extra musculature of an athlete's build—not '80s Russian women's shotput team "athlete" build, mind you—was no trouble either, as she was tall, near five feet ten inches. She distributed the bulk well, but retained a very feminine figure.

I never knew a soul who wasn't entranced with Morgan, at least when first meeting her. My grandparents were a rare exception. They barely tolerated her, though they were willing to "suffer" through the long weekends for my father's benefit. Their generation couldn't grasp what she was, but in all fairness, no one was really able to figure her out, so that was no fault of theirs. To everyone else, she was Wild Morgan, Irresponsible Morgan, Immature Morgan, Where-the-Hell-Is-She Morgan, Not Again Morgan, and on and on. But when we were here, she was all mine. Just Morgan.

"Hello in there," DeeDee says, pulling me out of my thoughts yet again. "I don't see a sign around here for 'Memory Lane,' but you sure seem to have found it. What are we going to do now?"

"Sorry, you're totally right. This whole place is full of memories, down to some of the rocks," I answer apologetically. "We're going to go around the lake to see if we have neighbors of any kind. The path is over that way." I point back, behind where we'd parked the truck, to the trio of steps that lead down off the driveway and into the heavily shaded woods beyond. Out of habit, I lock the truck as we pass it; someone can make out like a bandit from the stuff in the bed, but most of the weapons are in the cab and those are critical items.

The path runs off into the distance and then vanishes as it makes one of its turns a couple hundred yards into the dappled sunlight filtering through the aged pines. Those pines give their needles for the pathway, and one could virtually walk soundlessly as long as you watch out for the various moss-covered rocks that sneak from the surface, just waiting to turn a lazy ankle. That used to be one of our games, to split up and try to stalk the leader without sound while the leader walked and tried to hear the follower. While the tradition to stroll the path all together following lunch meant a single trip for grandparents and parents each day, it was rare when we children didn't circle the lake three or four times a day during visits.

On the right, as we enter the path, is the second most important thing we'll have here: the spring well. A tiny box entombed down low in the soft soil with an aluminum and wooden lid, it pulls from the spring that also feeds the lake to provide astonishingly clear, crisp, and (most importantly) fresh water. No more bottled water for us going forward.

We quickly reach the property line, marked by an orange-and-black-striped steel pole rammed into the ground. The stripes are for the Princeton Tigers, of which several of the family were. Not me—the grades weren't good enough, though Morgan had gotten in (of course) and turned her nose up at the school (of course). The distance between the other homes on the waterfront varies, but most of them are several hundred yards apart, with a few of the oldest ones set marginally closer together than that, though all are visually private from one another. Walking single file, eyes peeled, we make our way around the lake over the course of the next two hours, checking each house for signs of life—or unlife. Nothing. No cars in the driveways, no evidence of a single human or zombie.

The deep woods are cool and quiet, and at one point, DeeDee murmurs, "It's so pretty." She's right about that. It's as tranquil as I've always recalled and as I've been hoping it still would be. Crossing over a small bridge that crosses the outlet for the lake, we come back onto the same side of the lake as our cabins and one of my favorite other houses. It's a natural log, chink, and mortar house that sits high up off the water, with a wide porch and crushed gravel driveway.

What makes it really neat is a tiny island that stands only a few feet off the shore, boasting a solitary but tall pine growing next to a red-painted wooden bench. There's also a clever bridge arching over the water. As we pass in front of the area beneath the porch, I smell something. An expired fire. Not really fresh, but the hint of charcoal is in the air and makes me pause. We're still at least a half-mile on the path from our place.

I stop the girls with a gesture. I then motion them to stay where they are and to be alert while I circle the house and climb up the hillside behind it so I can see in the windows. Nothing in sight, and the rear door is firmly locked. Winding back around to the water side, I creep up the stairs to the porch at the edges of the steps to minimize any noise. There's a magazine discarded on the broad wooden planks, *Guns & Ammo*, but no other clue that anyone is home. Odd, but given how clear the air is up here, maybe it's just a whiff of the past, like someone else's burn barrel from months ago. Shrugging, I descend the stairs and rejoin the women, and we carry on back to our place.

Unfortunately, the location of the house key has evaded me during our walk, and I'm resigned to breaking a window in the main cabin. I can always repair it with a piece of wood or two; I'm sure there's some spare lumber in the garage. We pass the solitary stone chimney standing like a sentinel near the edge of our open space, a remnant of a fourth outbuilding that has been intentionally burned at some point in the way past for some unknown-to-me reason.

I unlock the truck to get the tire iron from below the driver's seat. I'm digging that out from among everything else we have jammed in there when Amelie pipes up from behind me, "I need to go to the bathroom. Really bad."

"Okay, just use the outhouse," I reply, gesturing with my elbow to the one unlocked building on the property. After all, what's someone going to steal from in there? The ancient Sears catalog that has forever been aside the seat? I've always wondered about that. Why have anything to read when it's virtually pitch black inside? Not like you're going to leave the door ajar for others to hear any sound effects.

"What's an outhouse?" Amelie asks. Really? She doesn't know what an outhouse is? I know the kids of today are pretty darn sheltered, but this is a little silly. I'm sure I hear a stifled giggle from DeeDee.

"That is," I answer, now pointing to the compact building, which is maybe four feet square with a pitched, green-shingled roof and a slightly open door. "An outhouse is pretty much what it sounds like, an outdoor bathroom."

She wrinkles her nose in disgust. "You mean we're going to have to go to the bathroom in that … that thing? Like, all the time, even in the middle of the night?" Good point. It's going to be a special trip in the middle of the night in the depths of winter in particular, but this is our life now.

"Yup. It doesn't smell. There should be some lime in the garage that we'll sprinkle in there from time to time to keep it as fresh as we can, but it beats marching off into the woods every time you have to go." Now I'm thinking this is pretty darn funny. Welcome to the country!

"So it's like a litterbox for people." Utterly deadpan.

"Now that you mention it, yes." Still with a dubious and slightly horrified look on her face, Amelie walks over toward the little hut. That's when it hits me. "Amelie, wait. I need to go in there first," I say as I walk toward her.

"Seriously? I have to go, like, right now, you know. Can't you wait, or go pee behind a tree or something like boys usually do?"

"It'll just take a second." I duck back into the truck, grab a flashlight, and flick it on. I edge the door to the outhouse open and then reach down under the edge of the board that the seat rests on to find the key hanging on a cup hook against the outside wall. Raising it triumphantly, I back out and show the girls.

"Um, yeah, thrilling. Can I go to the bathroom now or what?"

Knock yourself out. I have the key, we can get in, and we've found nothing on the recon.

We're home and we're safe.

Sure you are.

CHAPTER 6

We spend the next stretch of time getting settled in, unpacking the truck, arranging ourselves, and relaxing somewhat. One of the problems with being a threesome is that we can't separate when it's time to gather supplies. Despite the fact that we haven't found any signs of zombies thus far, there's no way we can split up. The main cabin is the best place for all of us to sleep, so I carry the mattresses from the two single beds out of cabin two and set those up in the family room off to the side. I sleep in my grandparents' bedroom, which feels pretty weird since it's a room I was barred from as a kid, so I haven't really seen its contents, ever. DeeDee stays out in the main room with Amelie, though comes in to sleep with me a few times as is her wont. We find a gas grill at one of the houses down the hill, along with several propane tanks, so we haul all of those back up in order to have hot food. Water is plentiful at the well, and we have the outhouse for the recycling duties. A number of the blueberry bushes are still bearing fruit, so we have fresh food for a welcome change. Memories of picking the compact, sweet berries flood into my mind since my grandmother sent us out to gather them in order for her to make one of her incredible pies during each visit. One for the bucket, three (or ten) for the mouth, and then green poop in the morning.

The weather remains pleasant, though the nights are cold—they always are, even in the heart of the summer. Sweatshirts and long pants are the order of the day for the morning hours when the sun is working its way over the hillside behind the property. Once it's overhead, the temperature creeps into the 70s and is comfortable enough to swim in the lake, though it's still very crisp, especially if you drop below the first few feet nearest to the surface. That's where we had always bathed in the past, so it's what we do now. It's not like we have other options anyway. It's glorious to be clean after months of the marginal bathing we did back in North Carolina, and we all take advantage of the opportunity daily. The little, yellow, plastic soap dish with a bar of Irish Spring is right there under the bench at the edge of the water, as well as an assortment of shampoos. You scrub from head to toe, dive into the sparkling water to rinse off, and then rest on the stone wall to let the sun dry you off. Amelie is shy about this, as expected since she's a budding young lady and swimsuits are in short supply, so she bathes and swims in a T-shirt and shorts, asking me to turn away when she's washing inside her garments.

DeeDee, on the other hand, continues to be DeeDee. Whether she's proud of her figure, is completely unselfconscious, or is trying to torture me (or all three), I don't know, but she insists on skinny-dipping every so often. One

more of the family's humorous signs is lakeside and declares "No skinny-dipping before 6 p.m.," but she's content to ignore that missive and happily strips down when the mood strikes her. Not that it takes her very long, since she mostly wears shorts and a T-shirt with nothing beneath it now that Jack's gone and she doesn't feel like she is being examined at every moment. So everything is freely moving around, and it's hard not to look. She's clearly aware that I'm aware and will sneak a grin at me any time she catches me. I'm a man after all, she's admittedly very attractive, and the last couple of months have been good to her. The hard lines around her eyes have softened, her hair has grown out so it cascades down her back in a dark, curly sheet that reaches her belt line, and the restricted diet and exercise of killing zombies has brought her musculature into beautiful definition beneath her skin.

After the first few times we all go down to the water to clean up and I watch her disrobe, I make sure to quickly undress down to my boxers and hop into the water fast and first since it's cold enough to keep things (mostly) under control. The cool air and invigorating water do their trick on her spectacular chest, which she, of course, will happily and casually display when talking to me as if we're having a cup of coffee. It's maddening at times, but in a good way since, at the end of it, she's fun to look at. Our physical relationship is unchanged from when we met—nothing other than her flopping against and across me to sleep. But now, with the absence of Eve, I wonder if that is due to change at some point, though I largely push that thought out of my mind. I think a full-blown relationship will complicate things, especially given that there's Amelie to consider. Who knows how she may react? Our existence is tenuous enough without mixing in anything that will interfere with the dynamic. It is, however, getting a lot harder to ignore the fact that my feelings for her are growing daily. She is comfortable to be around, funny in her bawdy way, optimistic, and kind. Qualities that are hard to overlook.

DeeDee, however, continues on her merry way as always. We're chatting about nothing in particular as we all lounge by the side of the gentle lake, though she's mid-chest deep in the water and idly soaping her breasts while talking. It takes an effort to tear my eyes off her as I sink deeper into the thankfully cool water and focus on the far shoreline, ever scanning for trouble or movement of any kind. Despite this, I can't keep my eyes from periodically flickering across her torso as she seems intent on scrubbing and being the cleanest in the history of womankind. Her faint pink, tiny nipples are fully (and impressively) extended as her fingers cross them repeatedly, and I'm about to lose my mind as I try desperately to keep my gaze away.

"It's okay that you look, you know," she says, interrupting my concentration about fat girls, sports, work, anything but her. "I don't mind it that you do. You're not like the other men that have been in my life, where I could tell they were thinking just about getting their hands on them and their dick in me. I think you're looking just to look, and," she pauses for a second before saying, "I think it's because you think I'm pretty. All of me. You accept me for me, and I've never had that kind of person in my life." She glances over at

Amelie, but she's napping on the bench, sprawled out in the sunlight like a giant, content cat. I wish I could sleep like a teenager, I really do.

"I've been thinking more about second chances, how we gave some to Jack but he couldn't change, and since he didn't, how you probably did what you had to do for the good of the rest of us back in North Carolina. I don't think we need to give up on second chances though, or on making whatever we can better going forward. You used to hear people talking about 'trying to do better,' but most of the time, they really didn't. I'm gonna just do better and skip the trying part, and some of that starts with me saying what's on my mind and being honest. People hid what they were thinking, most of the time, and I bet the world would have been a better place if they'd just said what they were really thinking, straight up."

I don't know what to say to all of that, except that I immediately agree with everything she's said. Wise girl, and I tell her so. "DeeDee, or do you want to go back to Diane? That might be one of the smartest things I've ever heard anyone say. You're totally right, about everything." I've always kept a large portion of my thoughts hidden from the world out of habit and because I have what I think is a horribly busy brain. At work, however, I'd at least tended to be direct to save some of the BS that was inherent on the unending hamster wheel that was corporate America. Changing those habits will take some effort, though I'm going to try … no … it's what I'm going to do.

"Nope, 'DeeDee' is how you really met me, so that's who I want to be. 'Diane' was probably gone the moment I started to grow up physically. Based on what you just said, does that mean you think I'm pretty?" She asks this question with a hopeful look in her lovely brown eyes, and I notice for the first time that the left one has a fleck of green shimmering at the edge of the pupil.

"It does. I think you're really attractive, both inside and out. I like you a lot. I have never met anyone like you, and I'm happy that we're here and together. I'm going to do like you said, just *do* and skip the trying part." I feel something of a weight come off my shoulders and notice we have drifted closer together during this exchange and are now not much more than arm's reach apart. It's like one of those cheesy movie moments where the male and female stars are backlit by an amazing sunset as they come together to kiss for the first time, eclipsing the sun with their joined faces. I have, however, always been bothered by how they lean in in one direction, but when the camera changes angle, they are turned the other. I have stupid shit come into my mind a lot.

We're not going to kiss though, movie-style or otherwise. Just as the silence has gotten to where I need to move closer and kiss the girl or go away and ruin everything, Amelie stirs on the bench behind us, awakening from her nap and stretching her arms over her head with a broad yawn. "I'm hungry! When's dinner and what are we having?"

I look at DeeDee with a wry grin and find her smiling back in the same way. It can wait. There's no way to know how things are going to turn out in these strange, new days, but this isn't something we need to rush.

CHAPTER 7

We're always preparing, collecting, and watching. I'm beginning to get a feel for what farmers' lives were like in the past—up early, working throughout the day, then collapsing in the early evening. Going to bed before nine o'clock is unavoidable and always has been. It's so dark and so quiet, and the days have always been hectic, so staying up late is impossible. Our lighting supplies are pretty limited in any regard; one of the things we've had trouble finding enough of are more candles, as they have clearly fallen out of favor over the years. I find that surprising, given the way that winter swats everything aside and dominates life here for months, but then I realize that this area by the lake is never used in the cold months, so being prepared for power outages isn't a need. The wind-up lanterns we've brought from the prepping store are fine, but, oddly, we don't seem to like the artificial light they cast, and so we use them only when needed. We'll be better served looking for candles down at the foot of the hill and in town where the year-round houses are located since those folks have likely been better prepared for periodic power outages.

We do find time to enjoy the pleasures of the location though, like swimming in the lake, taking a walk, patrolling the path, throwing darts against the ancient dartboard mounted on the garage wall, but our days are mostly occupied by a steady effort to accumulate more supplies. There's a shooting range across the way where I wanted to work with Amelie on her marksmanship, but we decide there's too much risk in gunfire drawing attention. She's an amazing shot at unmoving targets, but I want to dig out some skeet and see what she can do to mobile bogies whenever we decide it's safe to make a lot of noise.

The main cabin isn't exactly a fortress, nor is there a way to make it so, and in a way, there isn't much point in doing so either. If enough zombies come to chase us indoors, there is neither space to wait them out nor a convenient escape tunnel that will pop us out somewhere else on the property—I should know, having hoped and searched for one endlessly as a kid—so we agree to keep the house largely as it is. A few things need to happen, however, and most of that is relative to heat and the oncoming winter season. We bring as much firewood inside as we can handle to keep it dry and ready at hand. Winter's going to be nasty up here in the minimally-insulated cabin, and we're going to have to keep the fire roaring 24/7 to make it at least bearable. I'm worried about the smoke and smell, but I know we'll have to take the chance or turn into popsicles. We stack the wood on either side of the fireplace as high as I can reach, though I know that once we start to consume it, we'll have to bring more in on one side to dry out. We'll exhaust all we currently have if it's a typical cold season.

How to accumulate more wood?

We don't tiptoe around, though we do subconsciously keep our voices quiet and big sounds to a minimum. So far so good on the zombie-sighting front, but sound travels well across the water of the lake, so we see no reason to broadcast our existence. We generally keep things on the down-low. My grandfather had been able to summon Morgan and me for lunch from the far side of the lake with a shrill whistle that we'd hear no matter what we were getting into at the time. That rules out a chainsaw, which we *do* have. I sure don't relish the idea of hand-cutting any of the fallen trees in the nearby woods, hauling the pieces individually back to the driveway, and then splitting them with a sledgehammer and wedges, but I don't see a way around that. There are woodpiles near the other cabins, but a wheelbarrow is impossible to use on the path due to the multitude of creeping tree roots and mossy green rocks that all seem to grow from the pine needles cushioning the way. I can use the truck, but as the weeks pass, I've been reluctant to fire it up and make the additional noise. Not that it explodes to life like the Challenger, but it still firmly fires up like a proper Ford V8, and the exhaust snorts a bit and has to carry some distance.

I resign myself to working my way up the length of the driveway with the wheelbarrow and saw, taking the deadfalls closest to the road, stacking them on the driveway, and splitting them later on. The women are thrilled at this activity, really. It's hard work—my shoulders and arms are exhausted from sawing and tossing the cut pieces toward them so they can make the trek back to the cabin, over and over and over. I don't like splitting us up, even if it's only a quarter mile or so at first, but, otherwise, it's going to take forever unless I can find more wheelbarrows so we can haul the wood in tandem.

We've had something of a rainy snap over the preceding days, the cold precipitation chasing us indoors to keep warm and dry. This is the first time there has been a need for a fire to keep the chill from creeping its grasping fingers into the cabin, and I reluctantly start one after the women complain of the cold even though we're well-layered. Once the fire is happily crackling and popping the sap pockets from deep inside the old pine, keeping the sharply cool air at bay, I go outside to see how much smoke it generates. I'm pleased to note that the wood is burning cleanly and creating little visual evidence.

Small favors.

The three days have been filled with digging out some of the old games I played as a kid: Dominoes—with the very cool Chinese dragons on the back; cards to play War, Go Fish, Pounce, and more; and cribbage. I have to teach both of the ladies the games due to Amelie's digital-age upbringing and DeeDee's lack of any semblance of a stable youth. Amelie announces from her high horse at one point, "There isn't even an app for that game, it's so old!" But she settles down when I remind her there isn't an app for anything any longer.

Whenever we need a break from those, we work at tacking spare blankets to the walls and ceiling to preserve heat, hoping it will make some difference when needed. The windows are a weak spot for a number of reasons: they absolutely hemorrhage heat and are close enough to ground level that anyone, or any*thing*, can easily get in. But, after trying and failing to staple clear sheets of plastic over the outsides of the windows to trap heat—any breeze just grips and rips the plastic away from the surface and makes it impossible to see, like looking through a balloon—we do so on the inside of the house. It compromises our sight a bit for clarity, but it at least eliminates the escape of warm air. There isn't much doubt that we're going to be damn cold in the heart of winter, but these measures should help a little.

***

I'm alone, the girls having gone in the opposite direction from where I'm working, down over the rise of the driveway and toward the house with a full load of cut timber, when I see them.

Footprints.

Several of them in the muddy surface at the side of the driveway.

I glance around quickly and check the ever-present .45 at the waistband of my jeans, shucking my flannel shirt back on but not bothering to tie my hands up by working the buttons. There's nothing in sight, and I hear nothing except the faint sounds of the girls in the distance. Squatting down, I examine the prints. Boots, and from what I can tell, there

are three different sizes, with one set significantly larger than the others and creating a deeper mark in the soggy soil. These are clean impressions in the mud, not the dragging and shuffling that zombie feet tend to leave, so my thought is that these are human footprints. No way to determine whether they're men or women or a mix, except the big ones may have been a man's feet.

At first, I'm encouraged since more people means better security and firepower. My mind flips back to the faint smell of charcoal at the house down the lake from when we first arrived, and this all confirms what I've loosely suspected— we have neighbors. Neighbors who may have known we're here but have chosen to keep away for well over a month. That doesn't seem like a particularly good sign.

I move further along the driveway, back toward my place. The tracks end where the mud does, so I cross to the other side and find all three sets of prints again, heading in the opposite direction. So they came down the driveway toward the cabins and went back without coming to say "hello." Watching, and also not coming on the shortest route, which would have been the path adjacent to the lake. They didn't want us to know they were there. Super. I pack up the saw, my gloves, and my paranoia and head back down to tell the women.

DeeDee speaks up first. "Should we just go down and find them?"

"I don't think so," I answer. "If they went the way they did and then back, they clearly didn't want us to see them or know they were here. A little sloppy since they didn't check to see where they were walking and left the prints, but I still don't like that much. We're going to have to be alert since people will be less obvious than zombies, obviously."

"This is scary," adds Amelie, looking nervous and very much like the kid she is as she speaks.

"Yes, it is. No more separating, even for the short runs down the driveway. We've got enough wood for now, so I'll work on splitting it in the driveway. We'll all stick together, all the time."

That said, we settle down restlessly for dinner, picking at our soup and wondering what's in store for us. I have some ideas for how we can use my history here to our advantage, but if our guests are actual local residents, or very clever, it may not help.

***

The next week or so passes uneasily, with the days filled by splitting the massive pile of wood in the driveway, DeeDee restocking the lumber rack on the water side of the parking area, gathering what's left of the nearby blueberries, and scanning our area without appearing to do so. We suspend our walks around the lake for now—there seems no point in strolling directly into trouble, and the relative confinement bothers all of us. We have gotten used to the apparent freedom from zombies and have been enjoying the cabins like generations of my family did since near the turn of the prior century—relaxing, playing, and leaving the world behind. That the world we left behind is far more dangerous is irrelevant; this place sweeps everything away like it had

always done—cares, worries, and fears to the wind. That changes while we wait for something to happen.

Before I found the footprints, I had amassed more than fifty large slices of wood from the downed trees, so I have a minivan-sized pile to make my way through. I'm not wild about the sound that's generating from the sledgehammer against wedge since the sharp *tink* has to carry all the way across the lake. While there's no point hiding as they already know we're here, there's not much point in making any unnecessary noise, either, in case they're not the only neighbors. I set a few rags atop the wedge to limit the sound, but no matter what, a fairly large, rather in-shape man swinging a sledgehammer over and over is going to make something of a racket.

We all carried weapons constantly before this: me the .45 at the small of my back and the KNIFE in a mid-thigh holster at minimum; DeeDee still favors the crossbow—though I'm doubtful of its ability to kill a zombie, so I convinced her to carry the Glock as well; and Amelie has the rifle slung across her shoulders and a .38 that she isn't crazy about toting around but understands the need and acquiesces.

Luckily, my sense of smell is much sharper than I've ever noticed it being before, and I pick them up way before they come into sight—the odor of unwashed people wafting from beyond the main cabin and out of our line of vision. Working in New York City in my early twenties has gotten me far too familiar with that reek since the homeless and down-on-their-luck all smell about the same.

Smart. Coming down the driveway would have given us the sound of boots on gravel and the ability to see them from about a hundred yards away.

Not too smart, though, since they've skipped the higher ground … unless they've split up. Then we may have a problem.

As naturally and casually as possible, I set the sledge down against the chopping block and silently signal to the women. They move quickly, following the plan we've discussed each evening since the first footprints sighting. I pick up my shirt and wipe my sweaty face off, using the shirt as a screen for scanning back toward the cabin. I see nothing immediately.

DeeDee is wearing a baggy, light yellow, and rather thin T-shirt with nothing beneath. It's one of Morgan's that we've come across—she must have left it behind on a trip ages ago. It says, "Have a nice day" written on it and a yellow smiley face in the center, with a bullet hole dripping blood at the two o'clock spot. DeeDee takes a moment to fasten it further around her waist and knots it at her beltline, snugging the thin fabric tight against her chest and leaving very little to the imagination. I'm counting on the distraction to help us. God knows it's difficult enough for me to keep from looking at her when she's dressed like this, so I expect nothing less from anyone else with a pulse. I wonder idly if men become less interested in breasts as they get older, but I have a strong feeling that it isn't possible.

Finishing wiping my face clear, I slip the shirt back over my head and leave it untucked so the pistol isn't visible,

though it will be slower to grab if and when needed. We're going to let them come in and see what they want. Maybe I'm wrong and they're just shy.

They come into view around the left edge of the garage; they must have come around on the tiny, raised path made of small stones that's wedged between the house and the hillside's nadir. That was one of my favorite ways to sneak around on Morgan in the past, though we both knew about it, of course. It keeps you out of sight across the entire front of the cabin, the surrounding open area, and into the driveway.

There are three of them to match the footprints on the driveway and sized about as expected. All men, two of them looking like hardscrabble locals who made their living with their hands and bodies, knotty-muscled and without an ounce of fat to carry on their endless chores. Those two are relatively interchangeable, dressed in mustard yellow, grubby, canvas Dickie's pants, and flannel shirts. Their trucker-style baseball hats advertise farm equipment, and their faces are largely obscured by months of unkempt facial hair. They're both carrying rifles across their midsections, not in a directly threatening way, but more ready than they needed to be if this is purely a social, how-and-who-are-you kind of visit.

Trailing behind them by a few steps is the exception. He's big—really big—like six feet four inches and two hundred fifty pounds or so. He's got broad shoulders across a huge torso, complete with a belly swelling his own black and gray, tartan flannel shirt. He's wearing the same work pants as the others, but his beard is trimmed fairly neatly, and his shirt is tucked into his pants. I see the shine of a revolver glint on his right hip in a deep brown holster, but he's otherwise unarmed. No hat, but his hair is long and pulled back high on his head and bound at the nape of his neck. And, in spite of my misgivings, he's grinning.

The small group coasts to a stop about a dozen feet from where we're standing, with the big man settling in between his sidekicks directly in front of me. Clearly, this is the big man on campus, in more ways than one. I look him over as he does the same and size him up—dark hair, skin browned by a lifetime of working outside, wisps of red in his mustache and in the dense beard that covers most of his face. What's most notable are his eyes. They're small for his size and close together, and clever. Yeah, this feels like trouble.

Oh c'mon, this will be fine. I'm sure they're just dropping by with some baked goods. They look like nice boys.

"Well, hello there and welcome to our lake," he says in a booming voice that doesn't sound all that welcoming, though the smile stays on his face. I notice it isn't touching his eyes, however, which are busily scouring DeeDee's figure when he isn't looking at me. The other two have discovered DeeDee, too, and are clearly distracted.

Glancing over toward her, I see she's obviously uncomfortable under their scrutiny, but she's holding her ground.

I really don't want to start this off on the wrong note, but the way he referred to this place as *their* lake struck a nerve. Swallowing my first reaction, I bring a grin onto my face as well and hope it doesn't look as phony as it feels. "Thanks. We've been wondering when y'all were going to come on down and visit. We saw your footprints from a couple of weeks ago on the driveway up that way and were surprised to see we had some neighbors." This is when normal people should step together and introduce themselves, but no one is budging, and the three of them look at one another with a bit of consternation in their eyes. Obviously, they don't like the fact that we've known about them before they wanted us to know. One for us. I can't resist poking him in the ribs a bit. "Did your families have one of the cabins here like mine? We've owned this land going back to the early 1900s." Staking my claim to my turf.

"No," he says slowly. "Me 'n Jed and Elmer lived down in Stamford until all that shit with them zombies happened, and we wanted to get out of the town to somewhere quiet. Jed's daddy used to watch a couple of these places over the winters, so he knew 'bout them, and so we came up and kinda took over." Staking their claim to the turf.

"Have you seen anyone else? Or any zombies make their way up here?"

"Not more than one or two this year, and we took care of them, didn't we, boys?" he answers with a chuckle and nudges the ribs of the one to his right hard enough that it would have toppled a small tree. Rough laughs all around as whatever they'd done to handle the zombies come to mind, but they trail off pretty quickly and come back to focus on us. "Are you people planning on staying here?" he queries, beady eyes watchful under dense, dark eyebrows.

"Yes, we are. Like I said, this land's been in my family for over a hundred years, and it's quiet up here since, like you've seen, there's not much in the way of zombies. So I'm thinking we're going to stay here until … " I trail off because I realize I don't really have a concrete plan now that we're here. What *is* next? Do we just live up here forever? Do I expect something to happen that's going to kill all the zombies and put the world back together again? I don't have a clue, but that's a problem to be dealt with later. "I guess until whenever," I finish.

"Well, I'm not sure we're liking that idea, or, well, we're not liking the idea of *all* of you staying here. This is our place, we was here first, and visitors ain't welcome when you come down to it."

"What do you mean by 'all' of us?" I query, having an uneasily clear suspicion of which one of us they'd prefer is not here and which ones they'd not mind for company. I'm going to play dumb for a bit since, if they've got bad intentions, I need this to get a little out of hand so Amelie does what I need her to.

The big man pauses for a second, likely thinking about how to phrase the next thing that comes out of his mouth. "See here, the whole world is a fuckin' mess, so I'm just gonna say what I'm thinking straight like, but you're prob'ly not going to like it much, none of you." He stops, licks his lips, and glances at his companions quickly before refocusing on me after his eyes flit over DeeDee who's still standing to my right. I'm struck by his words being similar to DeeDee's when we were swimming, about being honest and clear in this new world, though her ideas were perhaps a smidge more innocuous than what's likely coming next. "You need to make a choice here, boy. The women are coming with us, to keep us … company during the winter. The way we see it, you can leave peaceful-like and our business is done, or things get ugly and you get buried on your family's property and the women still come down the way with us."

Well, at least we've gotten past the bullshit quickly. I know DeeDee has a frighteningly clear picture of what keeping these boys company will entail, but Amelie maybe does not. Everything's going to hinge on her ability to pull the trigger at the right time and find her mark. I have to draw this out a bit to ensure what needs to happen will happen, even if we get beyond an R-rated conversation. And I need to rattle our guests a bit.

I have to continue to push this some, so I figure I'd get right to the point too since we're all just being honest here. "That's quite a choice. I leave or die, and the women go with you to what? Clean the house, do the dishes, and cook for you?"

"Don't be a fool, boy, you know what I mean," he spits. I don't like being called "boy" much, but I need to keep my cool longer.

"No, I don't. You just said they're going to 'keep you company.' I don't get what you mean," I say, egging him on and seeing him begin to get flustered.

"I mean," and he hesitates again, "we're going to take your two women down to our place and we're gonna have them keep us warm in our beds, as much as we like. You know, you're startin' to make me mad. Don't make me take away choice number one."

"So they're just going to stay in your place and help you all stay warm? Oh, that's all. Okay, I get it."

He explodes. "You stupid fool! Stop fuckin' around! We're gonna bring them women down there and then we're gonna fuck them till we're tired of fuckin' them and then we're going to take naps and then fuck them some more. That one right there," he says, thrusting his chin at DeeDee, "she looks like she been around the way a good bit and might even like it, though ole Jed here's got himself a bit of an imagination. The other one, my guess is she's not been broken in yet, but we'll take care of loosening her up just right, won't we, boys? Where is she anyway?" Another nudge and laugh session.

DeeDee breaks in before I can answer, the anger seething out of her as she speaks. "You're not going to touch a hair on that girl's head, you sick bastard! Why is it that the whole goddamn planet has been taken over by zombies who want to eat every last one of us, and have done a damn good job of it so far, and you assholes come along, sticking to the same old stupid shit people have been doing to each other for forever? As for 'ole Jed' and his imagination, I stopped playing with little dicks in middle school."

I need to get a message to Amelie, who I hope is now utterly horrified, scared, and just mad enough to shoot, so I interrupt while the three men are momentarily speechless at DeeDee's outburst. "That *one*? She's probably taking a nap. You know how teenagers are. You probably walked right past her in *one* of the cabins on your way." I hope she's paying careful attention and not too upset to focus.

I remain standing in front of the big guy, and DeeDee is to my right in front of Jed or Elmer, leaving an open space to my left. "I'll tell you three something, though, I'm not going to go with choice one or two, but I'm going to give you a couple of choices and I won't ask this more than once. Number two, you leave right now, pack your shit, and get far, far away from *my* lake, and we'll call it quits. *One*, stay and die. You've got ten seconds to decide, starting now." I mime looking at the nonexistent watch on my left wrist and casually drop my right hand down to the hilt of the knife.

"Who the fuck d'you think you are giving us choices like you're in charge here, *boy*? All three of us have weapons, you ain't got no gun, the girlie here with the big titties only has a crossbow sitting at her feet that she'll never get to anyhow, and the kid is taking a nap. You're in no spot to threaten us. One city boy, one ex-stripper or something, and a girl who prob'ly hasn't had her first bleed yet." He steps in a pace or two closer, and his goons do the same.

Good. Take us lightly, Einstein.

DeeDee picks that moment to throw the ultimate distraction ... she yawns. Not a simple yawn, but a spectacular yawn, stretching her arms over her head as she does so. Men of any age beyond about fifteen in the old days know that this is one of the most foolproof things a woman can do to completely melt a man's brain—wearing no bra, a thin and tight T-shirt, and stretching one's arms over one's head is an absolute visual feast. DeeDee's breasts strain against her shirt, throwing her nipples into sharp relief in a way that no one can ignore. I knew it was coming, so I'm studiously *not* looking in her direction since I would have suffered the same fate as the three slack-jawed, back-to-puberty, speechless lumps who gape at her and give us our window.

It's over almost as soon as it began. Amelie fires the .22 from atop the rock that protrudes from the hillside like a flying saucer jammed into the rocky soil and overlooks the driveway, hiding her completely from sight at our level. I had hidden there more times than I could count as a kid and knew it made you invisible. The man at the far left of their line, in position one as I'd cued her, suddenly gains a small black hole in his face just below his right eye. He makes a small "huh" sound and drops to the gravel in a heap.

As the big guy tears his eyes from DeeDee and snaps his head around to see what just happened to his buddy, I draw out the KNIFE, hop forward, and ram it into his heavy stomach. The big blade sinks all the way to the hilt, and I lift with all my strength to gut him. Warm blood erupts, followed by a spew of internal organs and other fluids as the razor-sharp steel savages his torso. One of his hands grabs my forearm in a shockingly powerful grip and tries to pull the blade from his body, but it's too late. This is a very, *very* mortal wound, and his fingers quickly slacken as the clarity fades from those dark eyes and he, too, drops to the ground. The air sours with the smell of his bowels releasing. I try to tug the weapon free, but I get some resistance from a rib or something else, so I leave it where it is and spin to help DeeDee.

She's having a tougher time of it. Whichever of the two sidekicks is left is at least sixty pounds bigger than her and has the added advantages of fear and decades of using his body to make a living. In other words, he's ferociously strong. Despite her willingness to fight—and maybe some practice from past bar brawls—he's kicking her ass. That ends up being his undoing because he is completely focused on her instead of looking around.

Just as I slip the .45 from the small of my back, he strikes her a backhanded blow across her face that topples her to the ground with a cry. I'm quicker than him and raise the pistol to finish him before he reaches his dropped rifle. Amelie's even quicker than me, however, and the .22 spits sharply again from above and strikes him square in the throat. A .22 isn't exactly a weapon of mass destruction, but when fired from forty feet into soft tissue, it makes a superb mess. He falls onto his back, legs splayed to the sides, and the fight is *done*.

Adrenaline rages through my body, still looking for an outlet since I'm used to the longer conflicts with the massed zombies. I just stand there, breathing heavily in the now sudden silence of the aftermath. DeeDee slowly climbs back to her feet, nursing an angry red bruise that's already swelling on the left side of her face. I hear rather than see Amelie begin to climb down from her perch above the fray.

I step toward DeeDee who pushes me away, hard. "Son of a bitch! He actually took a minute to grab my boob in the middle of all that! I'm gonna have bruises all over the damn place. *Assholes!*" she hisses. She's as fired up as I've ever seen her, even more than when the zombies delivered her to Eve and me. Pacing furiously, clearly as flooded with adrenaline as I am, she steps to her attacker and kicks him hard in the balls, once, twice, three times a lady.

Mental note: do not make DeeDee mad at me.

Marching over to the inert form of the leader, she delivers a kick to his face. "Ex-stripper, my ass! I been a lot of things in the day, but a stripper wasn't one of them. Not that plenty of men didn't think I should have given it a try, but I can't dance worth shit."

She finally seems to be winding down and stops stomping around and faces me. I step toward her again, and, this time, she lets me fold her into my arms, carefully resting the unharmed side of her face against my chest. She releases me quickly though as we hear a stifled sob from Amelie. We both grab the teenager in a fierce bear hug. The ladies cry softly as I survey the mess. Lots of blood stains the dirt of the driveway and some of the big man's insides are spread out from his torso like an exploded spaghetti bowl.

Awesome. I'm going to have to clean this up. I'm not sure how good a zombie's sense of smell is, but it sure seems more finely tuned than mine. I don't want any chance of the blood drawing them here, so I'm going to need to get rid of that somehow, along with the bodies.

This was the best plan you could come up with? Not a "booby trap," but a "boobie trap"? Look at you, so very clever!

Listen, smartass, it worked, didn't it?

True, but you're going to have to up your game one of these days. Boobie trap. Sigh.

I herd the women back to the main cabin, DeeDee soothing the fifteen-year-old who has just killed not one but *two* human beings from pretty close in, rubbing her back and murmuring to Amelie. What a fucked-up world we have now. She should have been playing on her iPad, studying for school, thinking about boys or whatever else it is teenaged girls do instead of having to shoot men who otherwise intended to gang rape her. I'm not naïve enough to think that she doesn't understand exactly what they'd had in mind. She probably did when she was twelve, let alone fifteen, especially after I forced the big guy to describe things in such detail. They go sit on the front porch, and I return to figure out what to do.

"Need a hand with that?"

Oh for fuck's sake, what now? I still have the pistol in my hand—never even realized I hadn't put it back—and quickly raise it to hold it on the middle of three more guests. I first notice the middle-aged man with brush cut, graying hair. He's standing halfway down the graveled driveway I had fearfully ridden down on in a rickety, red wagon when I was a kid, certain every time that I was going to get dumped onto the rough surface at one hundred miles an hour. He's flanked on either side by magnificent canines: a Doberman on his left and a Rottweiler on his right. The dogs both tense at the sight of my weapon, but they don't move to attack.

"Easy, everyone go easy. Son, that goes for you too. You've got no further need for that pistol. I'm not here to hurt anyone, but I was ready to help if you needed it with those troublemakers, which clearly you didn't. I had that third one in my sights, though, until the kid took him down. Two good shots by her, too, especially with that little rifle." He has a commanding voice. Not one that makes you feel compelled to do something, but rather one that suggests it's okay to do what he says. He's heavily dressed in dark but weathered green and brown clothing, and a long-barreled rifle is slung over one shoulder, a giant rucksack over the other. His hands are empty and out to the side to reassure me … or lull me. But he could have taken any of us out if he'd wanted to, so that's something of a good start. I lower the gun and replace it in my waistband.

"Okay, kids, he's okay. Go see him," he says to the dogs, and I brace myself for a moment before seeing that the dogs' demeanor has changed completely with his command.

They trot happily over to me, tongues wagging to the side, and give me a thorough sniffing while I stand still with fingers closed to let them inspect me. I could do without the moment of panic when the Rottweiler gives my crotch a firm nudge with his massive snout, but they sit at my feet, seemingly satisfied, and allow me to reach out and scratch both knotty skulls.

"Sorry about Ajax. He does that to everyone. Not sure if it's a dominance thing or if he just got into the habit or whatever. The Dobie is Mabel. You can call me 'Top.'" He follows the dogs in greeting and reaches out a rough hand that closes mine in a firm grip as I introduce myself.

Now that I get a good look at him, I can see the additional lines in his face that put him somewhere in his later fifties. He's a few inches shorter than me, but moves in a way that's younger than his accumulated years that speak of a long career in the military.

"Mabel?" I ask. "Ajax is a badass name for a badass-looking dog, but Mabel? Not so terrifying."

"Oh, Mabel was my ex-wife's name. She was something of a furry bitch that'd just as soon bite you as lick you, so the name seemed about right. The dog is a lot smarter than the woman ever was, and while I'm not sure this Mabel likes me any more than that one did, she sure listens better and is mostly loyal, which couldn't be said about the woman." He says this with a wry chuckle, and I decide on the spot that I both like and trust him.

He explains that he's also been living at the lake for the past few months, but across the water and in a house deeper into the woods, away from the shore of the lake. He's seen the three men periodically, though he didn't bother greeting them as he'd seen no benefit. He'd noted our arrival, too, and had been waffling about coming to meet us. He scouted us from a distance while trying to make up his mind just out of an abundance of caution. As he scanned our shoreline via binoculars, thanks to the racket I'd been making while splitting wood today, he also saw the movement of the three armed men in our direction, so he'd double-timed it around the lake on the opposite route since he'd suspected they weren't coming over with a housewarming gift.

As we talk and I fill him in about our journey, we hoist the dead men into the bed of the truck, working with the familiarity of people who have known each other for a long time, moving in tandem without discussing what needs to be done. The biggest man is something of a struggle to hoist in with his buddies, but we finally manage to drag him up a pair of two-by-tens I'd found in the garage. If he catches any splinters from the boards, he makes no complaint. The dogs spend their time sniffing the dead bodies, marking their turf, and growling near the soaked-in bloodstains. We agree that digging it up and getting rid of the scent makes sense, so we haul out a shovel and mattock and set to adding that soil to the truck as well.

A low growl from Mabel tells us the women have cautiously come to see what's going on, and we make introductions all around. The dogs immediately greet Amelie and DeeDee after the okay from Top as they had me, complete with a thorough privates-mashing from Ajax. Top tells the girls he'd watched the fight and compliments Amelie on her marksmanship, explaining that he knows what he's talking about, having been an Army sniper in his earlier years before aging into desk positions. That explains the length of his rifle, which is several inches longer than our regular one. It's topped with a scope, complete with hinged lids on either end to prevent them from reflecting the sun and giving his position away when he's in the bush.

Speaking to DeeDee, he gives her some kudos as well for holding her own a bit against her attacker and then delivers an unexpected icebreaker. "Young lady, I'm glad I wasn't down here when you did that yawn and stretch move since, now that we're up close, I can see that my old man's ticker might not have survived it. D'you mind maybe putting something else extra on? Otherwise, I'm not going to get a darn thing done all day. I'm a bit of an old fella, but there's nothing wrong with my close-up eyesight." He says this gently and in a fatherly kind of way that can't be taken as anything other than honesty, and while DeeDee reddens (that's a first!) and covers her torso with an arm, she's also grinning from ear to ear.

And now we're four ... or six, depending on how you want to count things.

CHAPTER 8

eaving the dogs behind with the women—they'll happily provide a good distraction for Amelie in particular—Top and I drive the bodies down the hill and a handful of side roads until we find a spot at the edge of a dormant farm to dump everything out. The corpses *thump* to the turf and roll together in an unkempt little heap that I figure crows and other carrion-eaters will clean up over time. I hop up into the bed and sweep the bloodied dirt out as well; a modest burial of sorts as most of the soil ends up on the inert forms. To my surprise, Top mutters what sounds like a brief prayer. I catch something about "souls consigned to your keeping."

I ask him about that, having filled him in during the drive on the details of the conversation we had with the three men and what they were demanding, so I don't feel much like they deserve a heavenly landing spot exactly.

"Son," he begins, and I realize I'll have to get used to him calling me that instead of my name, which is fine, "everyone's dead, or pretty darn much near everyone. That wasn't so much for those three as it was for the rest of us, all of us,

It's a simple transition to a new normal, especially compared to the last time we added a person to the group—good old Jack. Top is a reassuring presence, and it's comforting to have added another fighter, a very real-world experienced one in particular, to our little family.

***

The weather starts to turn shortly after. Just a subtle shift in the breeze, at first, that now carries a hint of cool here and there, though the midday sun still feels sharp and hot on our skin. Luckily for Top's heart and my sanity, DeeDee recovers some of her modesty when bathing. She at least wears underwear and a T-shirt now, scrubbing discreetly beneath them.

The girls are floating out offshore on a couple of old inner tubes I found in the boathouse while Top and I are sitting on the edge of the stacked stone retaining wall that borders the lapping water along the entire frontage of the property. The dogs have been in and out of the water, but they're resting now in the grass with the radiance of the sun surely warming their mostly black coats. It's utterly peaceful with just a wisp of wind tossing the water, bright sunlight flickering off the miniature waves, and the quiet calls of birds. Just like when I was a kid, before Morgan's willfulness turned every family gathering into an inevitable hold-your-breath-because-sooner-or-later-something's-going-to-pop moment. I feel content, mostly safe, and as prepared as we can be for the coming cold weather.

the living and the dead. When you're in the service, a lot of us find that faith in a something—be it God or another deity or a thing—gets you through some scary shit. I've been in about every rotten, run-down, oil- or terrorist-producing shithole on this planet you've ever heard of, and some you definitely have not. Believing in something and being able to talk to him, her, or it when bombs are raining down on your position, or a hundred lunatic Hajis are hunting for your tiny squad in the dead of the night, got me through some nasty places in mostly one piece." He drifts to silence and gazes out the window at the passing green fields running rapidly to riot without the steady hands of generations of farmers that have tended them over the past decades.

I think about that as we wind through the countryside hills overlooking the valleys that dot this part of the state. I especially think about the men and women in the military branches, serving the country that seems largely made up of people who want to go first, get more of whatever than the next person, consume our resources selfishly and irresponsibly, obsess over the latest "It does everything!" gadget that actually does little other than distance humans from real contact with one another.

Not for the first time, I'm saddened. Those service people understand hard living, sacrifice, and doing things for the benefit of the whole. It occurs to me that they reflect the now-ancient values of our country not unlike the people who've lived here through nasty winters, dry summers, pestilence, and agonizing, endless labor. They had all toughed it out and lent a hand to friends and neighbors when needed. A mental salute to any of them that are still alive.

Curious about his name, I ask what his real one is.

"Top'll do. It's what people've been calling me for going on twenty years, and it's pretty much what I call me when talking to myself. You do that some too?"

You have no idea.

A friend told me a long time ago that there's power in a name, which I found interesting at the time. I don't remember the exact context of our conversation, but it may have been related to the names of the characters in a movie or book, how a "good" name made a big difference while a milquetoast one could actually weaken the character. Like anything in the past, some random phrases or moments stick with you for unknown reasons.

This current situation made that phrase come back to my mind, and now it makes sense. I suppose Top is entitled to reserve that power for himself in this ridiculous world.

***

We spend the next couple of days consolidating supplies from Top's cabin, which includes many things we already have: weapons, food, water, and one thing we do not—giant bags of dog food. Like, hoist-over-your-shoulder-and-haul-them-like-bodies-sized bags of dog food. I hope we have enough for them during the winter months because I can't picture the dogs slurping away at a bowl of soup or similar. Though, when it comes down to it, we'll all eat anything if we get hungry enough.

Guess that also means if you run out of people food, you may have to compete with a hungry Rottweiler or Doberman for their food. Good luck with that. You've seen their teeth, right?

There isn't much in the cabin that belonged to the Three Amigos that we can use—modest food supplies, maybe a month's worth, and a couple of large jugs of water. I wonder what their plan was for making it through the winter since it sure doesn't seem like they were prepared for months of confinement, and their stated ideas weren't going to fill empty bellies. Their place does have a massive stack of firewood resting underneath the deck, so we take the truck over for a number of trips and haul all of it back. We're out of room inside the house for the wood, but Top makes the suggestion to stack it around the perimeter of the cabin under the eaves so it will stay drier and act as a windbreak of sorts. By the time we're finished, it looks like a log cabin built by an insane person—tiny logs without mortar in the gaps stacked from soil to soffit. We leave the windows unblocked, however. Losing the line of sight is less preferable than a loss of heat.

At first, I think the sleeping arrangements are going to be a little compromised, but they're solved rather quickly when DeeDee just decides to sleep in my bed full-time. Top and Amelie will sleep on the mattresses in the family room with Mabel between them. We have the spare sleeping bag from our prep store shopping extravaganza, which turns out well since that's one thing Top did not have at his place. Ajax has apparently taken a liking to me and snores happily at the foot of my bed each night.

Top interrupts the moment, as if reading my mind. "This is a nice place you've got here. A man could be happy here for a long time, or, I guess, a man and his friends and his dogs."

"Thank you. It's been special to me since I was in diapers, just full of sharp and clear memories from childhood, most of them really nice ones. I thought we'd be far enough away from people and zombies to maybe have a chance to live some kind of normal life, and aside from the men, I think it was the right move."

He agrees. "You made a good choice. Winter's going to be shitty for sure. I grew up not too far from here and spent my first eighteen years getting through winters nastier than I care to remember. Soon as I turned eighteen, though, it was into the service so I could get out of here and find some excitement, see the world, serve the country. All that turned out okay, I suppose. Though, I'm thinking I could've done without that last bit of excitement with the damn zombies.

"We were stationed at a small base further upstate that's not on the map, a training spot for sniper teams since that was my thing, when the shit really hit the fan. Reports had been coming in from all over the world about the zombies. Bases were being overrun. Firefights were running so long that gun barrels literally melted as tens of thousands of zombies hit bases and swept through them like a modern-day Blitzkrieg. The military knows what it's doing, and we've got awesome weaponry, tons of training, and enough ammo to shoot everyone on the planet several times over. None of that helped," he mutters. "No manuals for what to do when a fucking horde of monsters, who don't seem to feel pain, don't die when you shoot them in the body, and like to rip people to shreds as they're eating them, comes over the hill. All the body armor, training, bullets, and explosives barely slowed them down. My guess was we got hit by two or three thousand of them. We had seventy-eight men and women on site. I was in an observation tower that overlooked the grounds and countryside during an exercise and saw them coming like a wave approaching the beach to sweep a sand castle aside. We were ready … well, we were on high-alert, but there was no way to be *really* ready for that. Fifteen minutes of insanity like nothing I'd seen in thirty years in the service, and then it was over. My tower was locked at the base from the inside, or they'd have gotten me, too, of course. I did as much as I could. Head shots, mainly, once I realized that was the key, but they just boiled over and through us and went on once everyone was dead."

I don't say anything, don't want to interrupt him, so I just nod as he takes a shuddering breath and continues. "We gave a fair account of ourselves. Must've been three or four hundred of those damn things dead outside and inside the perimeter, including a ton of wounded ones with their legs blown off or similar. Those were about the worst. Half a person crawling after me as soon as I came into sight, never stopping, even if they were down to just an arm, a chest, and a head. What the hell happened to make something like that, I don't want to know. I gathered a few more guns and ammo and marched around, shooting all of those ones in the head, one after the other, for *two hours*. I left after I came across some horribly-wounded soldiers who were beyond any help, and I had to shoot people I had eaten lunch with not a handful of hours beforehand. I've seen some crazy stuff, my friend, but it was all I could do to not just swallow a bullet.

"But I didn't, so here I am, back where I started. The dogs were ours on base and had luckily been in their kennels when it all went down. I let them loose and grabbed a bunch of rations for the three of us, and then we hoofed it in this direction. Doesn't seem like the zombies want to eat dogs, and those two are more than a match for anything on two legs. They have trouble killing them since their jaws aren't big enough to get around a skull, but the few we've run into have ended up on the wrong side of the fight, even when the odds were not in our favor, thanks to those two mutts."

I tell him the rest of our backstory, including details about the zombie queen and the one like her we'd run into (*hardy fuckin' har*) on the trip here. I also told him about Eve.

"That's a scary thought—ones that can think and tell the others what to do. Bad enough you can't stop them normally like a regular person, but special ones ... I don't want to think about that. The woman in Pennsylvania, though, what're you thinking about doing there? Been a bunch of weeks since you've been here, right? Maybe he's dead and she's on the way? Should we maybe all go get her, or you and DeeDee could go?"

I don't know, but it would make me feel a lot better if Eve were here and safe with us. She lingers in my mind each day, and I'm troubled by not knowing her fate, especially if there's something we can do. His nudge tips the scale, and I tell him so, figuring we could plan and pack over the next few days and then hit the road as a group, or split into pairs—or trios, depending on what the dogs decided.

In the end, though, Mother Nature takes that decision right out of our hands.

***

The early winter storm hammers across the region from west to east without us being aware of what's coming right away. Snow at this time of year isn't rare, but a blistering combination of wind, cold, heavy snow, and ice is uncommon. The precipitation begins the next evening, at first gently drifting from the dark sky and landing with a soft *tick* among the fallen leaves that have scattered across the property. Top and I are sitting on the front porch under the flickering light of a single kerosene railroad lantern, him smoking a horrid-smelling cigar, me idly scratching behind Ajax's ears as the monstrous dog happily rests his pumpkin-sized head on my thigh.

"This shouldn't amount to much, I don't think," Top opines.

I'm inclined to believe him since he'd grown up here in the fringes of the Catskills, and I'd been further south in New York, outside the City. Winter is a sour time all over the state, with what feels like endless months of gray skies, dramatic cold, and wildly varying amounts of snow. Great fun for kids, pesky for teenagers who want to get around—especially those well outside of the cities and in the hilly countryside—and a pain in the ass for adults. I recall a time when I was living at home in the Hudson River Valley suburbs but worked in Manhattan. I got up, went to work, came home, ate something, shoveled the driveway, shoveled the walkway, then slept. I repeated that process every day for four goddamn months. Great shoulder workout but little else.

We sit for a while in comfortable silence in the dark of the evening, just listening to the deep quiet of a world that has been shushed, and then go inside to join the girls for a game of cards. The rest of the night passes fairly quietly, with the occasional shudder of the house as a gust of wind pushes its way through the ebony blanket of darkness. It's nature's way of reminding us that it's very much in charge in these here parts, but it gives no other indication of what we'll find in the morning.

***

Top's weatherman skills turn out to be as good as his taste in cigars. Two feet of snow lies like a flawless quilt over everything in sight. At first light, the skies are clearer than a Caribbean bay, and the reflection from the sun is more than we can bear without scrounging up our sunglasses. The temperature has dropped such that a thin crust of ice covers the entire span of the lake—it must have stopped snowing long enough for the ice to form before we awakened. We bustle outside onto the porch after heating some water for tea over the fire. We're bundled up like kids on a snow day, just staring out at the perfectly white vista that sprawls in every direction.

Amelie and DeeDee are amazed; being born and raised in the South has prevented them from ever seeing winter's wrath unfurl like this. They got a few flurries, yes, and the periodic "storm" of five to six inches of snow every couple of years, but that was about the extent of it, and what arrived typically melted away within a day or two. This stuff is going to just be the base of what's to come, and we'll be lucky to see grass again before late April. Luckily, it's the lightweight stuff as opposed to the wet, clingy, and heavy snow that tends to arrive in the beginning and end of winter. Maybe I'll do well to climb onto the roof to clear the weight in any regard. I need to check and see if there's a snow shovel or two lying around since we're going to need it to at least carve a path from the cabin to the outhouse.

Great.

We're prepared from a supplies perspective; the question is whether we'll be able to get through it without going all Jack Torrance.

The dogs, however, immediately tear off through the snow like inmates freed from an insane asylum, barking wildly and racing around in great clouds of fluff until they're bearded, four-legged Santa impersonators.

Just like regular kids, I think with a grin.

***

An old saying comes to mind: "The only thing to do in Buffalo in the winter is drink."

As we discover over the next months, that applies to this part of the state as well, as storm after storm deposits what feels like endless snow to a final standing tally of nearly six feet on the ground. The bad part: one thing we're light on is booze. I'd been worried that we'd be mostly cabin-bound from the cold and reasonable snowfall, but I hadn't counted on being literally snowed in. Cutting walking lanes for the group's path to the outhouse has to happen almost daily, though we only use it for the longer-seated visits, with a bucket in the cabin's bathroom for making what ends up being a lot of yellow snow. A clearing also is required for the dogs, who, after the initial glee and novelty of the powder wears off, quickly do their business and retreat back indoors to curl up in front of the endlessly burning fire.

At first, I look at the thermometer each morning, through the ice-encrusted windows off the kitchen. Growing up in southern New York, I had plenty of respect for winter weather, and it had been a habit—pre-cell phones—to check what you were in for before going outside. Now, after about a week of seeing single-digit temperatures even in the middle of the day, I decide it's better not to know, and I'm so glad I couldn't see the gauge at night. It was depressing, and, frankly, walking outside for just a few minutes told me everything I needed to know.

How cold is it?

Fucking cold.

Or no-way-would-you-be-brave-enough-to get-naked-for-fucking cold, if you want to look at it that way.

The fireplace makes the house only barely tolerable. If you're close to it, that side of your body is pleasantly toasty, but the opposite side will be little more than just a little cold.

I doubt the temperature inside gets much above fifty, even on the rare clear days, and we all wear layers upon layers, including gloves, even indoors. If you leave the family room, you'll walk through a thermal change as soon as the fire's line of sight is gone, feeling the five- or more degree drop as soon as you turn a corner. There isn't room to move the mattress from the bedroom out closer to the fireplace, so DeeDee and I huddle close to one another every night to stave off the deep chill. Thank goodness for wool blankets, and I'm thankful as well in a way for the miserable cold—it easily keeps my mind where it needs to be when nestled against DeeDee and her alluring curves. At some point, Amelie and Top push their mattresses together, though Mabel still sleeps between the two of them (and under the covers), having by now adopted Amelie as her ward. Ajax is a smart dog too. He moves out of my room to a spot right in front of the fire. Top claims to be a light sleeper, so he volunteers to rise every couple of hours and add more wood to the fire.

About the only luxury we enjoy is bathing once a week, though the process takes forever as we heat water in large, Dutch oven pots outside on the grill, bring it into the bathroom, slowly fill the tub, bathe, and then reverse the process by scooping the dingy water out and emptying it outdoors. It's better than not getting clean from time to time, but I look forward to the lake clearing off and a full scouring from head to toe. I may even jump in there in April if it's clear, shrinkage be damned.

We all read books—everything in the cabin, including some of my childhood books like *Br'er Rabbit* and *Struwwelpeter*, a creepy collection of children's stories about what happens to you if you're bad, like having one's thumbs cut off with shears for sucking them. Not exactly the kind and friendly young literature of today's world—well, yesterday's world, though I stopped sucking my thumb the moment I had the story read to me a thousand years ago. I even think about writing a book myself, something to pass big chunks of time and exercise my imagination, but I can't come up with a storyline. Zombies? Golf? Zombies playing golf? It sounds like a lot of work, so I decide not to. Who would read it anyway?

A few games are in the built-in cabinets to either side of the fireplace—several decks of cards, which become dog-eared rather quickly as we all play more games from our youth and gamble for cans of soup or for who has to take the thunder bucket outside next. We all had to teach Amelie how to gamble, which, after a slow start, she ended up loving since there were actual stakes. She also seemed to be generally lucky with her cards, so she won often. As a result, she quickly picked up how to talk trash at the table, though her learning that part of it was actually kind of annoying. It's also possible I was annoyed because I was the one who lost the most, so I had to haul out the yucky bucket. Mature, I know, but picture handling a bucket full of other people's piss and shit and see how you feel when you get extra turns at it.

The dominoes keep us occupied for a while, as does cribbage, which Top at least knows how to play. It's too bad we don't have Risk or other time-consuming board games, but we'd only brought those with us when we visited and then took them home at the end of the trip. Top probably would've wiped us all out anyway at Risk, unless he's an unlucky dice roller.

One of the few reasons we leave our immediate area is to scout all the other cabins around the lake for books, games, *anything* to provide a diversion and occupy our time. The few books in our cabin, aside from the childhood books, are local history, and we all read those before the first month is out. Fighting our way through the drifts that obscure the path is honest toil, and I seem to be the trailblazer for most of these trips, with at least one dog behind me along with whomever else is bored enough for some outdoor time. It really does help to have four of us—not forcing us all to do everything together is beneficial. Good fortune does smile on us in one house. The owner must have been a Bernard Cornwell fan because they have his entire catalog, which is no small thing. I bring those back home and reread everything the historical military fiction master put to page, as does everyone else.

I find myself oddly content despite the lack of activity. I have never been one to sit still very well, constantly tinkering with this or that when at home, but the inertia doesn't trouble me here and I'm glad. One thing I do is fill a legal pad with to-dos since I know that, without a list, they'll turn into to-didn'ts. A ton of odds and ends like finding paint and stain for a few weathered spots around the cabins, roofing shingles, gathering firewood—since we'll be like squirrels, always getting ready for winter, even when it just ended—putting up some kind of barrier around the cabins, and anything else I can think of.

Physical exercise is a must, though, at least push-ups and sit-ups and so on. An observer would have found our "gym" hilarious if looking through one of the windows as we collectively break a little sweat here and there.

We do not see a single zombie through the winter, so there's that. I hope that any of them within a hundred miles are frozen solid and dead and stay that way so we won't have to contend with any except for migrants. I can't imagine that too many of them will be moving outside the larger cities, but whenever food runs out there, they're likely to seek it elsewhere.

Zombie female: *Muuuuuuuhhhhh!* ("Dear, let's move out to the country. I'm tired of the congestion and noise here in the city.")

Zombie male: *Muuuuuuuhhhhh!* ("Okay, that sounds nice. It will be good for the kids to have room to play. Where should we move to?")

Female: *Muuuuuuuhhhhh!* ("I was thinking upstate New York, kind of in the middle. What do you think?")

Male: *Muuuuuuuhhhhh!* ("Are you kidding me? No one moves *to* upstate New York anymore. What would we eat?")

Female: *Muuuuuuuhhhhh!* ("I suppose you're right. Let's move to Florida. It's warm and most of the people there move pretty slowly.")

It'll be good when winter's over.

CHAPTER 9

By the time winter begins to wind down, it has gotten quiet in the cabin for much of each day. We've all tried to keep ourselves occupied, but at the end of it, four mostly-bored humans with whatever percolated inside their heads, accompanied by two dogs—who are really beginning to smell like *dogs*—in a very compact and uncomfortably cold space for literally months manage to get up one another's ass from time to time. There are many snarky comments about who's going to cook, who needs to let the dogs out, who needs to remember to clean their feet when they come back in, etc. We're all going to be happy when the weather turns and we can separate a bit.

Spring, or what you'd call "spring" in this neck of the woods, arrives as abruptly as winter did. Over a period of a few days, there's a difference in the air, a hint of warmer humidity instead of the creeping fingers of cold that seek any gap in clothing or buildings, and the sun is out and strong. When the temperature creeps into the fifties one afternoon, we open the windows in the cabin and let it air out after months of confinement. Big dog farts in small spaces are not the best company.

Let's be honest now. Not all of those were the dogs'.

Anyway. Airing out was a good thing.

The icicles that ring the dripline of the roof are beginning to melt and drip incessantly, leaving deep pockmarks in the snowy surface below. The snowpack itself begins to settle and compact, and we're able to retire the shovels for the year as no new precipitation arrives. Our parking area turns into a muddy morass since it catches sun for a good portion of the day, which makes outhouse trips annoying because we have to walk across it, but we're all happy for a break and an opportunity to be outside more often than not. Nights still dive below freezing, which doesn't bother us as much since the sunny and warmer days are worth it.

Top and Amelie have talked military concepts over the course of the winter. She's fascinated by all his stories, particularly about shooting and how to adjust for the wind and distance and so on. He explains all about his rifle, which is one he has built himself and refined over the years— machining the barrel, carving the stock, and tweaking it to be as accurate as it can be. He teaches all of us how to break down and clean our weapons, his weathered fingers moving delicately and precisely across the oily surfaces as he talks to us without even looking at what he's doing. Amelie picks it up like a champion, her slender fingers dancing across the metal until she abruptly holds a handful of pieces instead of a gun before reversing the process and producing a pistol out of thin air. He tells her about being a sniper in the Middle

East, just sitting atop secure buildings every day and looking for trouble in every direction.

Anyone suspicious-looking was fair game—better to shoot first and be wrong than hesitate and get your buddies or civilians on the right team killed. I'm surprised to hear that since I have been under the impression via the media that the military isn't allowed to shoot without proof. I say as much. The only reply I get from Top is a long, direct look that says it all: Don't believe everything you read—we did what we had to do.

Once the ground is clear enough, he and Amelie start to go out daily to patrol the area, Mabel in tow, happily following them as silently as Top is teaching Amelie to be. They sweep in ever-widening circles until they're able to confirm that we're clear for a mile in every direction. DeeDee and I stay back, and within two weeks, we're surprised on the day the three of them return without us hearing a peep. I had seen Ajax's head and ears turn while I was cutting more wood, but I hadn't given that subtle move its due. No alarm was raised by him since they're "his," so I made a mental note to pay closer attention to the dog going forward. Amelie crept up behind DeeDee and goosed her in the back, bringing a shriek, followed by some language that made even Top's ears darken, followed by laughter, which was good for all of us.

Spring keeps coming, and we're able to open the windows and air out the cabin daily from the funk of six confined bodies trapped through the winter. The lake remains heavily frozen over and crusted with snow, and snow lurks underneath any shady spot, but any areas that get sun for more than an hour a day are rapidly clearing off. I take the opportunity one afternoon to dig out an ancient persimmon driver from one of the boathouse closets, scrounge up a ratty golf ball, and drill one clear across the lake. Ladies and gentlemen, meet the absolute, world-long driving champion. Well, maybe the crusty snow helped the ball roll. A little.

***

One evening, Top comes outside with another one of his nasty cigars to sit with me on the porch. We're comfortable in silence as I look over the vista, whose edges are fading from clarity as the sun travels behind the far horizon. I'm content and think we can stay here indefinitely.

Top breaks that reverie after a few minutes. "Son, me and Amelie have been talking when we've been out patrolling, and we're going to move," he says cautiously.

That gets my attention in a hurry, with memories of Jack spiraling to the surface of my mind like a torpedo. "What *exactly* do you mean?" I ask, probably more sharply than I intend, but Amelie is *my* kid to watch over and protect, and despite my liking Top immensely, he's still the new guy. I feel Ajax stir at my feet as he senses the sudden tension in the air.

"Whoa now, easy there. Maybe I said that wrong. We're not *moving*, moving. We're going to move over to the second cabin for sleeping at night."

"Um, still not a fan of the idea, Top," I reply, with the edge in my voice intended now. This is a fifteen-year-old kid we're talking about, and the rules haven't changed *that* much. I turn and face him directly, feeling adrenaline slide like mercury through my system—nostrils opening for more air and muscles tensing. Fuck flight, all I know is fight these days.

"Jesus, okay, son, slow down. I see where you're going, and that is *not* it," he says soothingly. "Sleeping is all it is. Separate rooms, separate beds, absolutely nothing more than giving us all more space after that shitty winter of being cooped up together. Since we've got the dogs to smell anything coming, and two pairs of us so no one is alone, it just made sense to us. I swear, my friend, that I have nothing else in mind and no intent to touch a hair on that young lady's head. If you suspect I do, go ahead and shoot me right here, right now." There's a bit of an answering challenge in his voice too. He probably hasn't backed down from anything in decades, and while he's being respectful of me as a man, fellow survivor and leader of our cadre, he isn't ever going to be a pushover.

I calm, slowly, as is my tendency, working to steady my breathing. Quick to flare, slow to cool. "Okay, sorry. I'm so used to protecting them, and after the shit we've had to deal with in the past and then from those sick men, I went somewhere I shouldn't have. As long as it's for sleeping, and Mabel is in the cabin, too, I'm all right with it." I know Mabel won't let anyone near Amelie at this point—she's like a mother hen. Well, if there is such a thing as a mother hen that goes around eighty pounds with a bad attitude and a mouthful of razor-sharp teeth, that is.

Top is no fool, nor is it likely that the dog wouldn't have gone there with them anyway, so he just nods at first and then adds, "Son, you shouldn't always expect the worst, you know."

I explain what had nearly happened with Jack and Amelie back in North Carolina since I don't want this to become a problem between us and he needs to understand where I'm coming from. His visage softens immediately and he nods again. "You could've told me that to begin with instead of going directly to pissed-off without passing 'Go.'"

"You could've been clearer at first, too, you perverted old coot." He laughs lightly at this, but it's a genuine laugh.

That seems to completely defuse things, and we remain where we are, Ajax settling as well. Things are going to be okay.

Aside from this little vignette, expecting the worst has worked out pretty well thus far. It's kept us alive and (mostly) together. My thoughts wander back to Eve, and whether she's survived the hopefully milder winter in Pennsylvania. I wonder if we should try to find her now that we've come out from under the bad weather. I also wonder if she's chosen to not join us on purpose, electing to follow her own path to whatever fate has in store. I miss her, no doubt about that, but I'm not certain whether it's because she was the first to join me and has been through so much with me already, or something more complicated. There's no way her father lived more than a couple of weeks after we departed, and there was probably enough time thereafter for her to make her way to the cabin before the snow arrived. I'm going to keep wondering for a while yet. Life has a lot more in store for us, and road trips are not in our immediate future.

CHAPTER 10

Like winter, I was never here in the early spring. We only visited on the long weekends that bookended the summer weather, so I never witnessed the earth reawakening in this part of the state. I long ago lost track of what month we're in; for that matter, I don't even know what day it is—my watch died eons ago, and I'd simply cast it aside at that point since time itself no longer mattered. Is it time to eat, sleep, or wake up? My body tells me these things now, and my guess is that it's a better clock than anything I've ever worn.

Eventually, the lake clears of ice, though not before an unpleasant discovery. Top, Amelie, and Mabel are off on one of their scouting sessions, leaving shortly after sunrise, and have been gone for most of the day. DeeDee, Ajax, and I are walking around the lake, idly passing the time while paying homage to routines of the past. We're armed as always and alert as always, but we're still sightseeing a bit as I point out the cabins of past residents, calling out the names that I can shake loose from my childhood's memory banks. One of the larger cabins is located near an inlet for the lake, where an ancient concrete and cast-iron spillway with an adjustable gate allowed control of the level of the water when needed in the past. It's also a haven for beavers, and I recollect memories of my grandfather mumbling about the "damn, brown, pieces of shit"—Grandparents cursed! What fun!—as he loaded one of his shotguns and marched off to take care of business.

Just after passing between the cabin and the shoreline, the path winds through the heavy tree growth toward a dark, wooden bridge crossing the shallow stream, perhaps eight feet wide. As is past ritual, I stop to look down into the water, even though it's covered by remnants of the deep ice. I have always been fascinated by still, clear water, even simple bodies of liquid like a puddle. No clue why, I just am. Today, however, the view is ruined by a face and upraised hands. A fucking zombie. Under the ice in *my* lake. A zombiesicle. A zombie who'd made it up here somehow during warm-enough weather, but then fell into the water before it froze, likely back on that night when Top proved he was unqualified to be a weather forecaster.

And we had no clue.

Damn.

I loathe the idea of that thing contaminating the water, even though it's arguably downstream from where we're hopefully going to be able to resume bathing once the temperature cooperates enough, or we get the stones to try some polar bear plunges.

DeeDee gasps as she sees what I'm looking at and asks if I think it's still alive. I tell her "no." We know zombies can't

swim, thankfully, and we also know they'll succumb to deep cold and die from either exposure or starvation—don't care which, re-dead is re-dead. This one is a male, with a typical angry-zombie-wants-food expression frozen for all time on his face.

Angrily, I stomp back to the garage that stands deeper into the woods than the cabin to find a shovel or axe or something else to break the ice so I can haul the corpse out. Finding a breaker bar weighing at least fifteen pounds, I mash through the ice, clamber down knee-deep into the water—and feel my nuts constrict like never before; forget swimming any time soon—and wrench the body out onto the bank. We each take an arm and drag it off further into the woods so we won't stumble on it during any other strolls. Ajax follows, grumbling low in his throat as he sniffs the body. It takes a few minutes. Frozen zombies are heavy, as in dead-body-filled-with-another-fifty-pounds-of-ice-and-water heavy. At least it's dead, but now the rules have changed. Again. We're going to have to raise our awareness level, and all of us will likely need to patrol on a daily basis. Like potato chips, you can't have just one.

We return to our cabin to find the others are already back and share our discovery with them. Pensive looks all around as we all digest the idea that our little corner of the world is not as remote and safe as we'd hoped. We agree to collectively be more on alert, and, in all cases, remain in pairs with a dog accompanying. From what Top has told us, the canines will pick up the odor of the zombies from several hundred yards away, if not more, so we'll be leaning on them for early warning.

***

The next few days pass quietly on a few levels. Top and Amelie are the main patrol team, staying out in the field for most of each day and sweeping in every direction to discover if any creatures are lurking. Amelie takes to this task like a normal teenager to a smartphone—she can't seem to stop, often rising before everyone else, prepping meals for their team (including Mabel), running down to the well to draw enough water into canteens for the day, checking her ammo and weapons, and then awakening Top to begin the day. Top tells me one evening that the kid is one of the best stalkers he's ever met because that day, she'd literally crept up on a deer from a hundred meters away, keeping downwind and out of sight until she was able to reach out and scare the bejeezus out of the animal by petting its back. He marveled at her patience, surefootedness, and utter silence when she moved. I can relate since she has taken to continuing her game of sneaking back home like a wraith and "getting" one of us almost every evening. I've learned to keep an eye on Ajax around the time they typically return and am able to surprise Amelie a few times when she's almost on top of me, but more often than not, we never pick up on her. It's creepy to not even sense her presence until it's too late. God help us if the zombies ever get more subtle.

Ajax, DeeDee, and I stay closer to home most of the time, me getting wood-cutting duty since I'm the ablest body for that kind of chore, though DeeDee carries more than her fair share of my work from wherever I saw and split any fallen trees I find. The nights are still cold enough to require a fire, and, if I remember right, the summer nights will need them from time to time as well, so this'll be a job that never ends. I do recall that a sweatshirt is usually the order of business first thing in the mornings before the sun creeps far enough over the hillside that holds the cabins in shadow until closer to midday. We'd hesitated about continuing the fire after finding the zombie, but we reckon warmth is more critical, and we've been burning it for months solid at this point without an invasion so it seems safe enough. Even though DeeDee nestles against me each night, as she's now done since forever, it's a rare evening when we can wear fewer than a couple of layers, even under the heavy covers. The deep, lingering cold reminds me why I moved south to begin with—I hate being cold. But since I'm pretty sure I would hate being dead even more, I figure this is where we're staying since at least we'll have safe months each year during the winter.

***

One night is kind enough to be mild. All of us are exhausted at the end of each day, either from the endless chores of gathering this and that or miles of patrolling. Without power, it's suddenly and incredibly dark once the sun falls behind the horizon. We're light on candle supplies after the short days of winter, so once the evenings arrive, we pretty much wind down and collapse in our respective cabins.

Today was bath day, which is nice since we accumulate a shocking amount of dirt and dust daily but don't want to use up the propane supplies by bathing more often than strictly necessary.

I'm nestled all snug in my bed, arms crossed behind my head and looking out the window at the early moon's reflection on the calm waters of the lake, which lights the room in monochrome shadows. The work of the day weighs heavily on me, and I know I'll be asleep shortly, caught in that space between alert and so tired that nothing can move you from the bed except for a disaster.

Out of the corner of my eye, I watch DeeDee strip layers of clothes off, down to a paper-thin pair of silvery, thermal underwear. I'm not sure how they provide much in the way of warmth since the fabric is stretched tightly across the curves and valleys of her lovely figure, but it's somehow a more alluring sight than when she'd skinny-dipped in the lake. The past year really has been good to and for her. The banshee who was delivered to Eve and me by the zombie queen, the one with blond hair and dark roots, weathered skin from exposure or tanning, a rough appearance from a life lived hard and fast, and a semi-fit body has been replaced with a pretty woman with a curtain of all-dark hair draped down her back, softened skin and visage, and a toughened body that displays in knots of muscle at her shoulders in particular, though she keeps a feminine shape. Silhouetted by the ghostly light behind her, she's a vision of the new world woman, tough and strong but definitely all woman. I tear my eyes away from the soft nub between her legs that the moonlight shows and let fatigue close them. I feel myself slowly begin to drift.

A few moments later, I feel her settle in the bed beside me, but instead of draping herself across and against me as usual, she just lies aside my body on her back. I'm not sure if she has something on her mind and wants to talk, but after some period of silence, I let the softness of the pillow embrace me and begin the final fall into slumber once again.

A sharp elbow into my ribs sometime later snaps me partly awake, which is followed by a mumbled "sorry," and I feel fidgety movement on her side of the bed.

"Are you okay?"

"Yep, sorry for bumping you. Go ahead to sleep."

"Are you sure? You seem like you've got ants in your pants over there."

Silence from her and the motions stop. It's much darker in the room now that the moon has risen enough above the eaves overhanging the door that leads onto the porch.

"DeeDee?" Now I'm coming fully awake, worried about her.

More silence from her side of the bed, but then an abrupt explosion of words. "Can't a girl just rub one out in peace?" she demands more than asks, exasperation clear in her voice.

No way did I hear that right. I must be wicked sleepy because if I wasn't, I think I just heard her say she was flicking the bean right here next to me. Nah, couldn't be. I must be sleeping already. Rolling over now.

"Well, can't I?" She sounds angry.

Always witty and ready, I come right back with, "Um …"

I feel the bedding shift heavily as she throws the blankets across me and gets out of the bed. I hear the soft pad of her bare feet against the wooden floor. Fully awake now but completely flustered by whatever the hell it is that's happening, I sit up, unsure what to do.

I see her go stand by the door to the porch, the faint residual moonlight barely illuminating her in the window. Her back is to me. "I'm coming right out and saying it. We've been sleeping in the same bed for months, and you don't touch me. I get it when Top and Amelie were here in the cabin, too, but they've been out for a long while. That day in the lake, when she was sleeping and you told me you liked me and we about kissed, that made me think, you know ...." she trails off.

Oh. Oh boy. I've spent so much time and energy trying *not* to be attracted to her beyond just admiring her assorted curves—you can't miss that unless you're blind—that I haven't really given any thought of late as to what's next, if anything. However, she's clearly been thinking ahead of me along those lines. Apparently not all of us have been spending our waking moments thinking only about surviving and what task needs to be completed next. Plus, we've been so cooped up over the winter months, it's not exactly been the ideal environment for what's-next-in-our-relationship thoughts.

"I'm horny, for God's sake! I touch you all the time, and you don't respond. We're together all day, every day, and all night. I look at you just as much as you look at me, though it doesn't take as long for women to see what they want to see as it does men. I've been waiting for you to do something, *anything*, to show me you really do like me, and I've about run out of patience and want to let the big knot of frustration out if you're not. I need something back from you for affection. Have I done something wrong, or has something changed about how you feel about me?" She sounds both angry and frustrated, which, given what she just said, makes a lot of sense.

So, let me get this straight. She wants me, she's utterly fired up and ready to go, and she also sounds just a hair pissed off at me. I'm a wizard when it comes to women. Okay, no, I'm not, but I think I know what to do now that she's basically hit me over the head with it and, in a way, given me permission to stop thinking and worrying, and I just go to her. I slide out of bed myself and go over to her, wrapping my arms around her from behind and burying my nose in her sweet-smelling hair. At first, her body remains rigid against my embrace, but then it softens slowly.

Not rushing anything, I turn her gently around in my arms and look at her upturned face for a moment. "I do like you. I do want you. I just didn't know the right way or time to say it. Come back to bed. I'll show you." I grasp her right hand and pull her with me back toward the bed.

The old me was always hesitant to make the first move with a girl, wanting to be certain she was sure about whatever happened next. That guy made it through the mess of the zombies completely intact, and while I've wanted to hold, kiss, and … um … do other fun things with DeeDee for a long time, I've been treading carefully. We have grown close through all of our trials, and I have strong feelings for her, but it always has to be right, in my opinion. Changing our relationship like this is a permanent thing, and there won't be any going back, which is why I've been a little anxious about this step. It seems, though, that this is about as right as it can be.

Once under the covers, we shuffle closer, allowing our hands to explore as we vanish into the ancient magic of a hungry first kiss. She is soft in all the places I am not, and the world fades away for a good long while.

CHAPTER 11

Luckily, there's none of the post-first-coital encounter awkwardness, maybe since the second and third had all happened in the same night. Afterward, I slept better than I had in ages, certainly back to before all of this. We all go about our usual tasks over the next days and weeks without a change, though at one point, Top catches DeeDee and I looking at one another for an extra few seconds, and I see something of a knowing smile on his face. No matter. He's a grownup too. We aren't overtly affectionate with one another after since we don't want to confuse Amelie in any way, though as it turns out, we probably should have given her more credit.

The nights aren't a whole lot different than they have been. DeeDee sprawls across me every night as always, but, some nights, the sprawling turns into a team activity if we aren't too exhausted from the day. I have never been a huge physical contact person, even to the point of preferring not to hug people whom I'm fond of, but after a couple of weeks pass, I realize something out of the blue: I'm happy, and I look forward to the moments where she and I will be alone, even if it's just a clasping of hands or a lingering look that hints it will be an evening with a later bedtime.

The warmer weather, such as it is up here, has finally arrived, and we're thrilled to resume bathing as often as we wish in the lake. The water is still damn cold, especially if you dip your toes more than a few feet down from the top layer. The first swim seems to signal the end of winter for good, and we begin to increase rather than decrease the firewood supplies for the first time in several months.

Amelie and Top return from their ever-longer daily patrols one late afternoon as the sun is beginning its descent behind the evergreen-lined horizon. Amelie seems strangely excited and doesn't even do any of the sneak-up-on-you games she's become so fond of. "Zombies," she announces as the three of them walk down the driveway. "Lots of them."

Shit.

Just when we were getting comfortable and back into the pleasant weather. I have been looking forward to all of the fruit-bearing shrubs springing into season, especially the scant raspberries that can be found if you beat the birds to them. Maybe I have been over-optimistic about how secure we'll be here, but I know we'll never really get away from the reality that 99 percent of the "people" who remain in the world are going to be ones who want to eat us. "Where? Close?"

"No, not close. They're more than five miles from here, back near Stamford," answers Top. He looks tired, as well he should if they've hoofed five miles out and back, with the back part of the trip under some kind of duress. "We were just looking for more weapons and useful things we could easily carry in the second story of one of the houses that overlooks the main road when Mabel tightened up and alerted us that we had company. After a minute or two, we looked out the window and saw a bunch of them basically just marching down the street from the east like a sick parade."

He continues, with Amelie nodding beside him. "I counted a little more than forty. It was hard to get an exact count since pairs of them were peeling off now and then to go into houses and buildings aside the road, so there was a constant coming and going. Regardless, there was a lot of them, and right in the middle of them was one of the ones you told me about. A cleanish one, less deteriorated, and moving more smoothly than the rest."

Another alpha. So it isn't just an isolated thing with the two we'd run into along the way. This really is everywhere. Not a pleasant thought. "Did they see you?"

Top snorts at this. "Son, they had no more chance of seeing us than the odds of the Yankees getting thrifty in the old days. We crept out the back of the house and along the side streets that ran parallel to their track and then up into the hills on the paths we've been using. They were sticking to the main road and looking for food. We know there is no one around, but I guess they're sweeping, just like we've been. The one in charge, it was a male, dark hair and fair skin, wearing some tattered, old blue jeans and a white, Dream Theater T-shirt, whatever that is."

At least this one has good taste in music. Still has to go.

Top goes on a little more. "They looked like they were stopping in town too. Maybe since it's the biggest one for a ways. Seems they're going to be thorough and go house-to-house like you all said they did back in North Carolina when finding the girls."

I see both Amelie and DeeDee shiver as they recollect the memory of being hunted throughout the subdivision.

"So it looks like we have neighbors, a shitload of them complete with a leader," he finishes with a grim expression on his face. He knows even better than I do that these odds are terrible for anything like a stand-up fight. We can maybe brawl our way through fifteen or twenty of them, especially if we see them coming and the dogs are engaged in the fight, but forty-ish is a big number unless we can get them gathered together and kill them en masse somehow like I'd done previously. Now if I only had a holocaust cloak, then I'd have something.

Top gives us a few ideas as to what to do next: we should stop the fire for now and no cooking—back to cold soup for us all for a while—anything to limit odors from our space. The road the zombies have been traveling is the only significant one through the area, and even though we're more than a mile removed from it, if they are being both systematic and thorough, they may just make the trek up the hill and find us. We keep close to our cabins now, though at least one pair of us (plus dog) makes the daily trek over the river and through the woods to town to see if there is any movement either toward or away from us.

Nothing changes.

They've clearly camped out there, and I wonder if they've found a pocket of survivors that we haven't and are able to stick around on that basis, or if it's the reverse—no food, but they aren't done looking. No encounters of any kind, though Amelie repeatedly begs Top to let her whittle their numbers down with his long gun. He admits to being tempted to allow her to do so since it would turn the proportions in our favor if she picks a dozen or two off without taking significant risk, but he reminds her that the first one or two shots from a distance are easy since the target is stationary and everything after that is chaos as they'd scatter and come hunting. If she goes down that way daily to knock one or two out, pretty soon they'd either stop gathering in groups or be waiting for us.

Whoever stays back is busy loading the truck with the essentials in case we have to bug out in a hurry. Water, food, a couple of propane tanks, most of the guns and ammo, blankets, gasoline, and so on are all placed in the bed since we'll be cramped with all six of us up in the cab—assuming all six will be able to make it if we're in get-the-fuck-out mode. I don't want to have to leave, but we won't survive a fight if a mob of this size finds us, so flight is the only choice. We could go deeper north into any of the innumerable towns all over the upper part of the state, and I'm sure we could find another lake and water supply and defensible building to live in if it comes to that. Maybe this is going to be the reality of the rest of our lives—run, find somewhere to stay for a while, run, and on and on.

Several days later, DeeDee and I are working on gathering some early raspberries from the bushes that edge the uphill side of the property, enjoying the fresh fruit but trying—like every berry picker ever—to put most of them into some tiny paper cups for Top and Amelie to share when they come back. The afternoon shadows are growing long from across the lake, darkening most of the property from the line of pines and other trees that border the lakefront. We're standing in the remnants of the sun, a residual sliver giving us the benefit of the late-day warmth.

It was Top and Amelie's turn to scout the zombies today, and they've been gone for most of the day, which isn't uncommon since the round trip is nearly ten miles to and from the town. So, even when moving steadily, it takes around three hours, and once close to the outskirts, we've been creeping over the final half-mile or so to an overlook above the center intersection. There has been nothing of note going on, which unfortunately includes no zombies leaving or heading in the opposite direction. We're pretty resigned to leaving, but we plan to initially head back south to go see if Eve has survived. Then we'll figure out an alternate place to stay afterward.

Mabel's harried barking is the first indication that something's wrong. I can tell she's no closer than the foot of the driveway off the main road, but the sound of her cries carries easily through the still-budding trees. Glancing at each other in alarm, DeeDee and I drop our cups and scoop up our weapons and haul ass up the driveway as fast as we can, scanning the woods on either side as we go. The cacophony continues as we run up the small hills near the end of the road that's covered in loose, natural stones and chunks of dirt, and I fear the worst. Coming over a small rise, we see Amelie and Mabel running in our direction, and fast.

I look beyond them for Top, but there's no sign of him.

Amelie is sobbing as she coasts to a stop, tears mixed with sweat and dust teeming down her face. The dog is panting heavily beside her. "Top … he … we … we have to go get him. They got him. I think. Maybe … we have to go get him," she manages to get out between deep breaths.

"Okay, slow down. Tell us what happened."

She heaves another few inhalations and seems to steady her breathing almost immediately thanks to the inherent fitness of youth. Then she tells us what happened.

They were just leaving from their scan of the town when a dozen or more zombies emerged from near the side of the trail we've been using. Mabel got a wild hair or picked up the scent of a squirrel or similar animal, so she had bounded off into the undergrowth a couple of minutes earlier, but they were used to that and knew she'd rejoin them shortly. The zombies had very obviously been lying in wait until the two of them were amidst the group that was secreted in the bushes at the edge of a field that leads to the narrow entrance of the trail. Then they erupted to attack them. From what she managed to explain, she and Top killed a few of them immediately, and Mabel came howling into the fray to keep several of them occupied. However, as they were close to being overwhelmed, Top threw his rifle to her and screamed at her to run, escape, and take the dog as he waded into a group of them with both a pistol and knife, giving her a precious moment to escape. She hesitated only long enough to see him take several more down before disappearing in a tangle of limbs, cursing, and zombie moans, and then she sprinted away, followed by the dog.

I look down at Mabel to see that she's spattered with crimson all over her previously ebony coat, and I know she'd been a monster in the middle of the fight, doing anything she could to protect the girl. Just like Top had done. Shit.

Amelie insists we have to go back for him, right now, but I know there's no chance he's alive, and even if he is, he has to be grievously wounded or possibly even on his way to being one of them. She fights us both, crying hysterically at the loss of her mentor and companion these last months. Both of the dogs whine at her misery, and DeeDee finally manages to get her to allow a long hug for some small solace. Amelie is covered in blood and gore herself, and we coax them both back toward the cabins and lake so we can get them cleaned up, with nervous glances over my shoulder the whole way back.

This is bad. I feel terrible at the loss of Top and admire him, again, for sacrificing himself to save Amelie. He was a steadying influence on all of us, patiently teaching us what we could learn about woods craft, weapons, and tactics over the long winter, not to mention giving me some male companionship. He really took the girl under his wing, and she clearly looked to him as a father figure, who is now just as dead as her real father. Not good. We have to leave, and quickly since nothing good is coming, especially if the goddamn zombies are setting up ambushes and obviously know we exist.

Night is falling rapidly. I join the women at the water's edge near the bathing area and pull Mabel into the shallows to get her scrubbed off. Oily, red blood and whatever else had been caught in her coat sluices off to float on top of the water in a rainbow slick, flickering in the setting sun. Ajax sits on the shore, looking around and making uneasy sounds in his throat. DeeDee soothes Amelie and slowly strips the soiled clothes off her, dropping them into a heap on the stones on shore. I finish rinsing off the dog and call her and Ajax to me, walking away to give the women the privacy they deserve and to give me a few minutes to think and scout, though the dogs are not on alert.

I don't want to leave now; it's getting dark, and we still have some supplies to transfer into the truck since we've only loaded non-essentials and will have to gather more water from the spring, the rest of the weapons, the sleeping bags, dog food, and other odds and ends before we can saddle up. I resolve that we'll leave first thing in the morning, and I'll stay up as a guard for the night to prevent any surprises. As long as one of the dogs is near me, likely Ajax since I'll bet Mabel will sleep right on top of Amelie tonight, I should be all set.

The girls come up from the water, Amelie wrapped in a thick, yellow towel and looking both young and old at the same time. Her eyes are red from crying, and water from her damp hair drips to mingle among her tears. The strain is evident on DeeDee's face. She'd really liked Top, too, and I can see the fear as well. We've had a quiet and peaceful winter despite the miserable cold. We thought we were safe here, and the hard reality that we've lost someone we cared for and are no longer secure is tough to digest.

DeeDee shepherds Amelie toward the main cabin, but the girl insists she wants to sleep in the second cabin, the one she'd been sharing with Top. I nod my assent. Even though I'd prefer her back in the main cabin with us for the night in case she needs something, if she wants to be alone and mourn on her own terms, we should let her. After all, she'll only be a few dozen steps away. Mabel pads softly behind them, so at least she won't be alone. I light one of the kerosene lanterns on the porch so DeeDee can find her way in the gloom.

Some twenty minutes later, she reemerges, shutting the screen door quietly and walking through the night to join me. We sit on the pair of rocking chairs furthest from the second cabin, Ajax at our feet.

"I think she's okay," DeeDee says softly. "She's exhausted and just strung out emotionally, but I finally got her settled and down to sleep. Poor thing. She's just a mess, saying she should have stayed with him and fought, even though I told her she'd be dead now too. That was her last comment before she fell asleep, that she wished she had stayed and didn't care what would have happened. Jesus. What a fucked-up mess."

I can only nod. This version of the world is unfair enough for adults, let alone children or near-children. With so few of us left, any loss feels disproportionately savage, and having lost Eve and then gaining and losing Top weighs heavily on all of us. At least I'm mostly able to compartmentalize things, focusing on what's next versus what has been done; you cannot change the past, but you can do better in the future.

After telling DeeDee my plans, I urge her to try to get some sleep, promising that if I start to drift while standing watch, I'll come get her to switch with me. She agrees and steps in close and hugs me hard, and then she wordlessly goes indoors. The dog raises his head to watch her, looks at me as if understanding we're staying up for the night, and then he lowers his giant noggin back on his paws with a grunt. After a moment, however, he rises and goes to the door leading inside, turning back to me for assistance. I figure DeeDee could use the company—especially if the dog senses that is the case—so I let him indoors and return to my post in the rocking chair. I sit after putting out the lantern to preserve my night vision and listen to the sounds of the night, senses as alert as they've ever been. Of course, I eventually fall asleep, but, of course, I don't even notice.

CHAPTER 12

I did my share of sneaking out of the house as a kid. Not to get into any specific mischief, but rather just for the challenge of doing so without being caught and also for the freedom of being out of the house and awake after my regularly-scheduled bedtime. We lived so far from anything that there was nowhere to sneak to unless Morgan arranged for one of her friends to come collect her, or, if I was lucky, both of us. Those nights were both exhilarating and frightening since, if we'd been caught trying to leave the house so late, we'd have been grounded for something close to forever. But hanging out with her and her older, fascinating friends was enough of a lure to get me to tag along whenever invited. Most of the time, we just went for drives to anywhere and then hung out, the older kids passing a bottle around and laughing while music played from the speakers of whomever's car we were in. We'd creep back just as silently as we'd left, sometimes just before dawn. No one the wiser.

I start awake the following morning with the mother of all neck cricks plaguing me from sleeping in the rocking chair all night. I have no clue when I drifted off, nor how I was able to sleep outside in the cool evening without waking, but, somehow, I did both. It's barely daylight. The sunrise is fully hidden behind the hills to the east, but it leaks enough light so I can see to the fringes of the property until the details fade in the first few steps of the riotous undergrowth that creeps to the edge of the open areas. Gingerly rotating my neck to loosen the cramp, I stand up quietly so as to not wake DeeDee—there are some generations-old creaks in the porch flooring no matter how carefully you move—and move over to the front door. Ajax is there, waiting for me, stubby tail wiggling his hindquarters, so I let him out. He promptly goes to do his business and then meanders over to the second cabin, sniffing this and that along the way until he trots up onto the small porch and sits at the door, releasing a quiet whine—Rottweilers don't exactly "whine," mind you, but more like a grumble in the throat; of course, it only sounds marginally less terrifying than their actual growls.

"Ajax, come here. Don't wake Amelie up," I say quietly. His head turns toward me and then back to the door. "Dude," as if the dog knows the distinction between command and coercion, "over here, let's go." I snap my fingers, but he continues to ignore me.

Then it hits my sleepy brain: he wants me to let Mabel out. So I walk over and quietly step onto the porch, hoping we can avoid waking Amelie and allow her some badly-needed rest. However, I needn't have bothered with tiptoeing. The screen door is the only one that's closed, and no one's inside.

Gone.

Both the dog and the girl.

I fling the door open and cross the first room in a couple of strides to the second. No one there either, and only the bed in the main room is unmade. Where Top had slept. Okay, she slept in his bed, but now she's not here. No guns in sight, nor her backpack that carries her spare ammo, canteen, snacks, and so on.

Shit. Shit. Shit!

Gone, baby, gone. You know where to, or where, too, haha.

"DeeDee!" I howl as I burst back through the screen door, somehow minding to not blow it clean off the hinges—countless reminders from Grandmother—and yell her name again as I race onto the porch of the main house and call Ajax to me.

A groggy DeeDee appears at the front door, wrapped loosely in a sheet and blanket, hair mussed. I skid to a stop, my running shoes squeaking on the painted boards as she cracks open the glass front door with a questioning expression on her face.

"Amelie," I say, "she's gone, Mabel too. I think she's headed back to town, either to find Top or take some of them down or both." I'm mentally doing the math for how long it will take me to run, and I mean seriously haul ass, the five miles along the paths, and what the chances are that she's already there or if I can catch her on the way. "Shit! I've got to go, *now*, and I've got to take Ajax with me in case there's a fight and I need better odds. Are you okay to stay here?" All of this spills out of me as I nudge past her to grab my shotgun, the .45, several spare clips, the KNIFE, and a partly filled sports bottle.

She just nods and gestures me toward the door, getting out of the way. "Yes. Go, just *go!* Save her, please …" she pleads.

"Ajax! Come on, boy! Let's go!" I sprint off the porch, keeping in mind to duck at the eave that has threatened to decapitate me for decades once I was tall enough. Hitting the broad stones of the walkway, I race off up the driveway with the dog trailing me, hoping I'll have the wind to keep it up for the whole run and praying I can catch the child and save her.

The route to town leads mostly through the woods once you clear the driveway, which winds through heavy shade like a green and brown tunnel over the loose gravel and soil separated by a mossy middle hump where tires haven't flattened paths over the years. It's cool under the trees and silent except for the sounds of our feet and my breathing.

I'm not really a runner, but more so a stubborn jogger in the old days. For me, speed wasn't the goal, but rather endurance and the length of the workout. So, while I can run for a fairly long time and up to about ten miles on a good day, I'm not fast.

Today, I need to be fast, so I urge every ounce of speed out of my body since I'm only going to have one shot at this. I desperately hope Amelie has taken it easy and is walking. I also hope she hasn't been gone for long. If the zombies were smart enough to be waiting for her and Top the day before, they damn well are going to be smart enough to be waiting again for seconds, or worse, they could have been backtracking them. Their sense of smell is clearly enhanced, as evidenced by the queen giving the women the sniff pregnancy test back in North Carolina.

My feet pound in a staccato rhythm, and I focus on keeping my breathing as steady as I can despite the added burdens of the guns and water bottle.

Once out on the lake access road, I follow that for another half mile or so down toward the more level ground of the valley, and then I dodge into the opening of the path that parallels the main road leading back into town. Branches slap across my face and torso as I blast along, mindless of the scratches, just focusing on running, running, running. Ajax trots heavily beside me, and I hope the big dog will be able to maintain the pace as well since Rottweilers aren't exactly known as racing dogs. Even though we've all been on the current Zombies-have-destroyed-the-world diet, he still has to go one hundred twenty pounds of rock solid, furry muscle. I've long since stopped wearing a watch, so I have no idea how long we've been running, but I know we're about halfway to the town when I coast to a stop for a moment to take a quick slug from the water bottle and give a splash to Ajax as well. As we resume, I hear the one thing I'd hoped not to hear.

Gunfire.

A quick volley of sharp rifle shots spaced close together, but evenly, which imply she's picking from multiple targets and has time to choose, fire, and aim for the next one and fire again. I picture her methodically choosing targets and swinging the rifle down a line of bogies to eliminate. So perhaps there was no ambush by the zombies, which is something, but we're still at least fifteen minutes from reaching the town. Fearing we have no chance, I tear off again, sprinting now with what little is left in reserve and not worrying about breathing other than sucking in as much air as I can. My lungs protest against the effort, and I wish we'd been able to be more active during the long winter months so this would have been easier.

More gunfire and now the faint sound of barking carries over the hills as we close the distance, but the shots are closer together and less organized. I just run and hope and run.

Ajax finally gets tired of my human pace and barks once as he leaves me behind. I don't know if the dog will make any difference, but if he can, more power to him. No shots over the past minute is a horrible portent of what I'm afraid I'm going to find, and all I can do is hope she's running away, preferably in our direction. I can't believe Amelie went without us, no matter how attached she was to Top, especially knowing the zombies terribly outnumber us.

I'm dying from the run. Five miles of trail-running at full speed is undiscovered ground for me, and sweat pours out of every pore in my body. My shirt is soaked, and my legs are beginning to get jittery and less cooperative, my knees wiggling treacherously with every step. I've had nothing to eat today either, so I'm running low on fuel as I emerge from the depths of the path and into the meadow that separates the woods from the edges of the town where houses are more sporadic and petered out. Ajax is standing on the far side of the grassy space, just standing and waiting for me, but I can see his hackles are up and he's on high alert. I drink the last of the water as I stumble to a walk and toss the bottle to the side to free my hands.

There hasn't been a sound now for several minutes, and I fear the worst.

Moving more and more slowly as I close in on the dog, I look in all directions for signs of danger. Ajax hasn't budged, and, as I make it to him, I see why. He's standing next to Mabel's body sprawled across mashed-down grass, her blood staining the emerald blades from what looks like dozens of injuries. She isn't moving, nor is her chest rising and falling even slightly. Three zombies are scattered and down nearby, none of them moving either. One's arm is torn nearly completely off, and I can see as many bite wounds on their corpses as are on hers, so I know the dog had given a ferociously good account of herself. No sign of the girl, but from the signs of trampled greenery, I can follow where the fight had raged across the open space. I pat Mabel's flank and say a silent "thanks" to her for protecting Amelie.

Passing three more inert zombie bodies sporting single bullet holes in their faces, one right through the eye, I keep going, following the blood trail. Ajax follows, right on my heels and grumbling deep in his chest.

Taking a chance on sound, I shout, "Amelie!"

There's no reply.

There are two more bodies face-down in the grass with exit wounds gaping from the backs of their shattered skulls, and then I finally find her.

I don't know what waits for us after this world, if anything. Maybe it's a peaceful, idyllic place, where there are no zombies, plenty of food, and shiny, happy people. Maybe it's something else, or maybe there's nothing.

I drop to my knees beside her slender, teenage body, letting the shotgun spill out of my hands. She's dead. There's no question about that from the injuries I can see, but her head was spared from any damage, and somehow she has a beatific, content expression on her pale face despite the way she must have died. There are a couple more of the abominations piled off to the side, so by my count, she and the dog had taken down around ten of them. I can barely move, just reach out to her face and let my fingers slide down her cheek as I start to cry hot tears of sorrow and anger. A kid. A goddamn child.

I sit there silently for a few minutes, unmoving with the breeze drifting across the field and drying my clothes. The dog waits, too, without a sound, but then he stands and walks away. I watch him without thinking, but, subconsciously, I notice he's tracking something since he's snout down and casting. He gets about forty yards away before he stops and pops his head up to look at me in that curious way dogs have where you think they're trying to tell you something. I don't move … or can't move, whichever. Finally, Ajax utters a snip of a bark, so I rise and bonelessly walk over to see what he wants.

It's a body, a fresh one, though there's almost no flesh remaining on the skeleton; there's just some sinew holding everything together. Blood has splashed the grass in a sloppy, crimson circle around it, soaking the ground in some places. There are over a dozen dead zombies with gaping head wounds, sprawled in every direction, some as close as a few feet. I stand stupidly, looking down at the corpse before realizing that this must be Top since I now see what remains of his pack to one side, torn to shreds with the contents scattered, and one of his boots discarded a few feet away.

Fuck me.

I haven't ever stuck around to see what a horde of them did to someone when they brought them down, but I'm not prepared for this. It's like locusts picked him clean. What little water remains in my stomach suddenly rebels and spews out, leaving strings of vomit trailing from the side of my mouth. He obviously fought like the devil to the end, buying Amelie and Mabel time to escape. Thanks to him, and Amelie and the dog's work this morning, the zombie population must have been halved. I see one of his pistols on the turf, so I pick it up, rack the slide, and check for ammo. Good.

I can't leave Amelie behind for this. No way. I make my way back to her; we'll find the right place to bury her near the cabins. It's going to be a miserable trek back, but somehow I'm going to make it happen. I sling the shotgun and the sniper rifle over my shoulders and then reach behind her shoulders and knees and lift Amelie to my chest, shifting her weight and knowing I'll have to stop often. Just as I get settled and ready to begin, I sense Ajax come to attention next to me, bristling into a growl deep in his barrel chest.

Muuuuuuuhhhhh!

They pour out of the trees that shade the perimeter of the meadow some fifty yards or so away, summoned by either Ajax's bark or my call to Amelie. It's not a shambling, shuffling, stuttering zombie walk either, but a steady, slow jog. They spread out like a fan as they emerge. Five … six … more and more until I see over a dozen of them coming at us. More than I can handle in a fight, even with the multiple weapons here at hand, especially since I'm exhausted from the run, wrung out emotionally, and not likely able to draw enough anger up for a proper brawl. Also, I can't outrun them if I'm burdened by two long guns and Amelie's body. I'd be caught in half a mile at most. Decision-making in split seconds these days is the difference between living and being dinner, so I do the only thing I can and gently place Amelie back on the ground.

"Please don't let them eat her up too," I ask whatever may be listening. I loathe the idea of leaving her, but there's nothing for it, no choice, and I have to make it back to DeeDee so we can get the hell out of here.

I take a second to take some shots with the rifle, dropping the pursuers at both ends of their line with a single shot each. I turn to run into the woods behind me, but I stop short. Two large zombies, both male, block the path not ten feet from where we stand. Raising the rifle again, I aim at the one on the left, just like I'd taught Amelie, and squeeze the trigger, almost moving the barrel sideways to the second one before completing the motion that ends in an unrewarding *click* as the gun comes up empty.

Shit.

I drop it to the side and just charge as I draw the KNIFE with one hand and the .45 from the small of my back with the other. Squeezing off a wild shot, I hit one of them in the shoulder and spin him around while Ajax tears into the other like nothing I have ever seen or heard. I think zombies are turned to rage at all times, but the dog makes them look like a toddler having a temper tantrum. He's fully ready for battle, snarling his challenge as he launches headlong into the fight and moves in a horrifying blur of anger and brutality. The zombie never stands a chance as Ajax knocks him off his feet with the collision and then proceeds to rip body parts to shreds with the carnage of a machine gun at close range. The finishing touch comes when the dog darts in and closes his slavering jaws on the zombie's neck, severing it completely in a wet snap as he twists his own neck in a savage yank.

The raging dog is ready for more and spins back to face the oncoming group with a bellow of invitation to come meet the demon who will gladly provide them passage to Hades. That pauses the line for a split second in instinctive fear of something more terminal than they are, but then they surge forward again. I'm awfully glad he's on my side, and I want to fight, too, to avenge Top and Amelie and find an outlet for my own now fully-blown fury. I briefly think about making a stand here, but the image of DeeDee alone and waiting for us flickers across my mind, and so I call the dog to me. I scoop up the rifle and fire Top's pistol into the face of the downed zombie as we pass and speed into the woods, fatigue be damned. We have more than enough adrenaline to get us home.

The trip back feels like it takes forever as I run like a zombie—staggering, unsteady, and wavering on the path as the adrenaline unwinds from my system and leaves me disoriented. Luckily, I'm able to make something better than a jog since that's max speed for zombies. They'd manage that, but anything faster looks like a comedy skit as their focus on the goal (food) gets in the way of their ability to see obstacles, so they would constantly run, trip, fall, rise, run, repeat. More than once, I, too, fell over an upraised root on the route as I wasn't able to lift my leading foot high enough over the obstacle and went sprawling headlong only to rise and continue. My body is drained like it has never been, just tumbling forward to keep moving like a puppet whose strings are tangled. A friend who was a real runner told me that during his first marathon, he lost track of it all; time, where he was in the race, everything, but he just kept moving forward on auto pilot and followed the runner in front of him until someone told him to stop after crossing the finish line. This is what that must have felt like, though I have no one to follow. However, no sound follows us either, which is a relief since I'm not sure I'd do anything other than lie on the dusty path and let them have their way. My mental state is no better—two of my people and one dog dead in less than twenty-four hours, and suddenly we're half the group we've been. Amelie's young, peaceful face keeps rising to mind, torturing me for not watching her more closely last night and for falling asleep when I was keeping guard. The fact that the dog missed her escape, too, is no comfort.

Finally reaching the head of the driveway, I pause at the "One Way" sign to catch some semblance of breath and look back down the sloping road and adjacent fields to ensure I'm alone. I am, so I begin to walk the last stretch, knowing that DeeDee has to be out of her mind with worry by now. A normal round trip to the town takes more than three hours, and while I've been running as much as possible both ways, it has likely been that long today too. I wonder if the gunfire carried this far, and if so, what she has made of it. There's no way for me to move any faster—trudging up the sparsely-grassed center section of the road is all I have left, and I'm thankful to have a downhill go the rest of the way after I manage to reach the peak of the driveway a few hundred yards in. I'm desperate for something to drink, and I visualize just resting on the edge of the lake and sticking my face in to take a deep draft.

The cabins come into view and along with them the sight of DeeDee on the front porch, the crossbow on one side of her and a shotgun on the other. Shotguns remain the weapon of choice for the zombies, and I continue to load all of them with alternating rounds of buckshot and slugs since, if it happens to be a buckshot round, it will cripple one or more zombies in a group and you can finish them off with a handgun or the following slug. The damage that a solid round inflicts on a less solid zombie body is spectacular, usually tearing massive pieces of torso out or removing limbs in a spray of gore and bits and pieces.

DeeDee comes to her feet as I wander shakily down to the foot of the driveway and taper to a stop. She looks over my shoulder and then back to my face. "Where's Amelie? Mabel? Top?"

I can see that she anxiously wants an answer other than the only one I can give her. I just shake my head slowly.

"No. Nonononono." Her shoulders droop, and she raises her hands toward me at first, then across her chest and then back down at her sides.

"I'm sorry," I say numbly. "I got there too late for her and the dog. They were already gone, and Top was definitely dead yesterday like we were afraid of. They took a ton of them down, at least." That sounds weak and of small solace; words aren't going to do it, so I step forward to enclose her in a hug, trying not to let my exhausted body flatten her. I need rest and some water.

"But ... she was just a teenager," comes her muffled voice from my chest.

She and the millions of other dead teenagers all over the world, courtesy of the epic all-time prank that has been pulled on the human race, not to mention every other age group wiped from the surface of the world. It's never going to make sense. "I know. And I had to leave her there. I didn't want to, but a bunch of them came out at me and the dog, so we had to get out. I don't think we were followed, or if we were, it was from some distance if they can track us. I think we need to leave—and soon."

I suppose it still makes some sense to go try to find Eve, for lack of any better ideas or any other destination. If she's still alive and at her house, it's a sign that it's a fairly safe area.

Right now, however, we just need to get out of here and go anywhere. "DeeDee, I need some water, and I have got to sit down for a minute. Can you work on loading the rest of the stuff into the truck?"

She nods wordlessly, breaks the hug, and walks back to the main cabin. I follow her part of the way and find one of the large canteens on a side table. Plopping down heavily into one of the rocking chairs, I drink the cool water and feel it run all the way down to my stomach. Ajax pants his way over, too, and I pour some into my cupped palm for him to partake as well since we have no outdoor bowl for the dogs—they preferred the lake water, anyway. Sated after a couple of minutes of sipping my way through the full canteen, I close my eyes for what's supposed to be just a second.

For the second time today, I start awake. The slamming of a truck door is what wakes me, though "awake" is a strong word for it. I'm incredibly groggy and disoriented, literally barely aware of where I am. Naps have never worked for me unless they're for several hours at minimum. Power naps are no such thing in my case; I'd wake up even more cranky and out of sorts than before sleeping, so I have avoided them. I try to focus my thoughts, but I don't have any luck.

DeeDee comes around the side of the garage with a harried look on her face. "I was worried about you," she says. "You've been out for about forty-five minutes, but you didn't even budge when I walked past you a bunch of times. I wanted to leave you sleeping, but I'm done. We can go, but the truck won't start. Not even a click. Maybe the battery is totally dead?"

This is shaping up to be one miserable, shit-ass, fucking day.

The truck won't start.

Something nibbles at the back of my mind, but finding anything in there is like trying to herd butterflies in a hurricane.

The truck won't start … the winter … we haven't driven it in a few months.

There we go.

I took the battery out and stored it back in the main cabin for the cold months for just this reason once the first heavy snow arrived. Now if I can only move through the fog that's trapping me in this chair.

"It's indoors," I manage to croak. "I'll get it."

"No, I'll get it. I know my way around cars. You just get to the truck and bring the dog." Ajax is awake but sprawled at my feet, probably just as crapped out as I am.

Somehow, I get my hands on the armrests and get to my feet, continuing the shuffle walk over to the truck. I was tired on the trip from North Carolina, but now the fatigue hangs over me like a three-hundred-pound blanket. I open the back door and boost the dog into the rear seats, and then I haul myself up into the passenger side up front, slumping against the comfort of the cool leather without bothering to close my door. DeeDee returns with my weapons and a fresh canteen, and then she goes back in again. When she comes back out, she's holding the heavy battery with both hands by the carrying strap across the fronts of her thighs, the weight of it bouncing against her legs as she goes.

"Hey, pop the hood would you?" she calls.

I lean over and trip the catch, but then I just lie there across the seats.

Yellowjackets are fairly innocuous creatures. They mostly do whatever it is they do besides fly around and tend to flowers, but they largely exist without bothering humans much unless you're unlucky enough to (literally) stumble onto one of their nests in the ground. That can get exciting as they pour out of the hole to defend their turf and repel the intruder. I've been stung here and there over the years, and, of course, the initial sting is unpleasant, but then it fades away within a day or so.

Yellowjackets are fairly innocuous creatures, unless you are allergic to their sting.

The brief shriek from the front of the truck doesn't immediately get me moving. It takes a split second for it to register, and my first thought is that the zombies have followed us. That does the trick. I bolt upright, groggily grab my gun and hop out of the truck, not noticing the dense buzzing sound at first while I scan our perimeter and see nothing before coming around the edge of the raised hood to find out what caused her cry.

DeeDee lies on the ground, moving weakly, with a horde of yellowjackets crawling on her exposed skin like a moving black and yellow cloak. Her skin is peppered with angry-

looking, raised, red welts already the size of golf balls, and I see more of the insects pouring out for the assault from a hole in the driveway just inside one of the front tires of the truck. The buzzing is ever-louder, and I move as quickly as I can, lunging down to scoop her up roughly and ignoring the bugs who redirect their wrath to me, though I feel dozens of stings within the seconds between picking her body up and rushing to the fringe of the lake just thirty feet away. It's going to be cold, but it should shed the bugs, so I just jump off the retaining wall and into the shallows at the shore. I wade out until we're in a couple feet of water and drop DeeDee, pushing her gently under the surface while covering her mouth and pinching her nose closed. More of the little bastards find me and take their revenge, and my skin starts to burn. I drop into the water with one hand supporting DeeDee, and the yellowjackets finally leave, their mission to discourage their attackers complete.

Dripping water and shaking from the temperature, I gather DeeDee into my arms and walk heavily back to shore, hugging her to me tightly. The welts are slightly smaller, but there are so very many of them, and her face is a mottled mess of swollen tissue. I call her name, desperate for a response, but she's barely moving and doesn't respond, though her eyes flicker open and find mine. I see the sorrow in them match my own as I realize she must be in deep pain … and horribly allergic to bee stings.

Frantically searching my memory banks for the contents of the single medicine cabinet in the house, I try to recall if we have any antihistamines, even long-expired ones. When we'd stopped at the prepping store, we'd grabbed a few first-aid kits and had also accumulated assorted antibiotic creams, bandages, and even some needles and fine thread for stitches if needed. I don't think we have any allergy-type medicine, but I carefully place her in the sun on the stones at the top of the retaining wall and tear off to the house, banging open and nearly shattering the glass door. I reach the bathroom and explode through the medicine cabinet to no avail. There's nothing there.

I race back to the truck, heedless of a few more bites from the still-angry bees, and rip open one of the kits. Nothing but a tiny packet of ointment for insect bites to reduce the itching. Knowing this was pointless but not about to give up and lose her without a fight, I run back, fall to the ground next to her, open it with my teeth, and smooth it across her face, watching her eyes desperately darting around as she fights for air through a swollen throat. I hold her again, crooning soothing sounds and begging her not to die, but I feel her motions slow. I pull back so I can look at her directly.

We sit there in a pile on the mossy turf, rocking gently in the cooling afternoon and holding eye contact. I don't know what else to do other than give her comfort, whatever little I can provide. Her breathing becomes even more unsteady and shallow, and I see a tear fall from her left eye and drip down across one of the bumps to trail off into her hair.

"No. Don't leave me, *don't*. I can't do this by myself. I need you."

She shakes her head faintly, her eyes never leaving mine, but they flutter and start to close.

"DeeDee! DeeDee!" I shout. "Don't you give up. Stay with me. Please ...." Her eyes close, open once more, and then she takes a few shuddering breaths and is finally still. "*No*," I moan.

Gone.

All of them gone, and this is by far the worst.

At least Top and Amelie had gone down fighting and somewhat in control of what happened. DeeDee is the victim of stupid chance and whatever genetic flaw that gives her the allergy. Fucking yellowjackets of all things. After a year and then some of surviving zombies and hunger and winter, she's brought down by insects. I raise my head and howl my rage at the sky, furious with whatever's up there pulling the strings that her second chance had been ripped to a stop far too soon after it had begun. She deserved better.

I'm alone now. Three of them torn from me in just over a day. Grief pours out of me in an endless torrent of bitter agony. Yesterday morning, there had been the four of us. Now there's just one.

I sit there for who knows how long, just holding her and crying, crying, crying until the sun falls behind the tree line. Ajax comes over and nudges me, whining as he then nuzzles DeeDee's shoulder, clearly not understanding why she doesn't respond, and that breaks my daze. Not alone then; I have a dog. His soft, brown eyes gaze into mine, and I wonder, not for the first time, at what they really think if anything other than food, sleep, affection, and the world is their outhouse.

A man and his dog. How sweet. A man, his dog, and a .45. Kinda sounds like a country song. Easy solution, a little murder-suicide, and it's all over. You can put this whole thing behind you.

Piss off. You are exactly what I don't need right this second.

The practical side of me wants to bury DeeDee right away, just something that formalizes things. It seems like the proper thing to do. The problem is that in order to make any kind of actual hole in this rock-filled soil, you'll need dynamite or heavy equipment. As kids, Morgan and I tried to dig holes for whatever reason, but we would quickly quit after no more than a couple inches since there was no damn point—you may as well try to excavate with a toothpick for all the progress you'll make.

I rise, heaving DeeDee up with me. I see the woman under the swollen skin and flash back to our "introduction," when she was delivered to Eve and me by the zombie gang back in North Carolina, the rough-edged, foul-mouthed harridan, and how she was the big advocate for second chances, even with Jack, while living her own second chance and becoming a more content person. Of all of us, she earned a better ending.

Stumbling a bit under her weight and the accumulated fatigue of the day, I carry her to the furthest cabin. I don't have a better idea, so I just lay her on the bed, bring the covers up to her shoulders, and smooth her wet hair off to the side so I can see her face clearly. I just stand there for a bit.

Are you going to say a prayer or something? Sure, there's a God, with a severely fucked-up sense of humor.

Who or what would I pray to? If there is anything in charge of all this, it can kiss my ass. The world is dead, my people are dead, all of them—blood family and now my new family. All dead and gone. I'm not praying to anything.

But I do have something to say. "Thank you for being you and for being part of this … this second chapter with me. I won't forget."

I leave the cabin, closing the door on my entire new life that closed the door on my entire old life.

CHAPTER 13

After that, I just wander aimlessly around the property, Ajax trailing me. I bump into memories and ghosts alike, every piece of everything being a part of the past, some more distant than others. Like a writer who's stuck on which direction to follow in a story, I'm in a limbo between recalling what was and figuring out what to do. Over the course of my entire life, I've reached into the past for comfort during difficult times, and more often than not, I've found myself here in my mind, touching these pieces of my history. Now there is little solace to be found as the poison of the present takes charge. At one point, I find myself sitting in the front seat of the BMW in the garage, surrounded by the familiar smells of the building, the car, and the history of me. If I knew anything about cars, I'd get this thing running and just drive somewhere, but it's as dead as everything else.

Later on, I sit with my feet in the lake, just watching the water and the tiny fish below the surface, darting about without a care. The thought beckons again that I can just end it with a single shot, like a mermaid calling a sailor to oblivion, and I do raise the gun to rest it beneath my chin to feel the cool metal and smell the oil. One small tug on the trigger, and it will all be done. Not right now though.

Night falls with me sitting numbly on the front porch on one of the ancient lounge chairs and its slippery, floral-print cushion. As it has always done, it claims me to sleep.

***

Morning breaks cold, and I open my eyes to find that the dog has clambered up onto the lounger with me, which keeps us both warm enough though makes for awfully tight quarters.

I wonder if he did this because he was seeking warmth, or because he wanted to provide comfort. I'm sure he can sense my misery, as he hasn't left my side since I "buried" DeeDee.

Steam rises from the utterly still, mirror-smooth surface of the lake, obscuring the far shore. It's a beautiful, peaceful sight that I've seen almost every morning I have been here, and it will keep occurring long after I'm gone. Ajax gazes at me with caramel-colored eyes. Such gentle, brown marbles in his majestic head. Who will take care of him if I end it? It has taken me a long time to realize this about myself, but I have recognized that one of the things that drives me is to take care of and help others. Not in an I-should-be-a-doctor kind of way, but just doing small things in order to make things easier for others has brought me contentment and happiness. Watching him watching me tips the scale. "Dog saves man," in the headline of the daily paper that no one reads.

I'm not going to take my life, nor am I going to leave. This is my place, my refuge, and if I'm going to die, it may as well be here. If *they* find me, then so be it—I'll take a lot of them with me on the way. The memories, old and new, will be here for me. I'm not going to quit or run. I'll stay right here. Maybe Eve still lives and will come. Maybe Morgan is a survivor and is making her own way across the country to find her share of peace here. Maybe there are others.

I decide I can and will live with the ghosts and memories.

One really is a lonely number, isn't it? Want me to sing the song for you? No? Well, you'll always have me, at least. I'll keep you company forever.

I sit on the front porch of what I've always thought of as my grandparents' cabin that overlooks the small mountain lake. My shotgun rests against the dark, wooden railing in front of me, and one of my well-used .45s is on my right thigh. I've got a tumbler of Old Granddad one hundred-proof whiskey close to hand, though no rocks and no twist. The dog sits with me, curled at my feet in a glowing finger of sunlight. A bunch of other guns and weapons are scattered around on the tables and chairs of the cabin's porch for when they come.

I am waiting.

I am ready.

I am alone, as I was in the beginning.

ABOUT THE AUTHOR

GREG RODE

GREG RODE is the author of the *Sanctuary Chronicles* series (and a children's book he hasn't quite figured out what to do with yet). He lives in Cornelius, North Carolina with his family and two small dogs that would be of no use whatsoever when the zombies come. He used to live next to the golf course described in *Shotgun Finish*, but has moved twice since then. The zombies followed him anyway, which is a good thing since they keep him out of trouble. He is still not a very good golfer.